WITCHES SAIL IN EGGSHELLS

Chloe Turner grew up in London and then Bath, attending St Paul's Girls' School, London and Clifton College, Bristol. After reading Archaeology and Anthropology at Churchill College, Cambridge, she qualified as a chartered accountant. She now lives in a village near Stroud, Gloucestershire, with her family and some chickens. Chloe won the Fresher Prize for short story in 2017, and has twice been awarded the Local Prize in the Bath Short Story Award. 'Waiting for the Runners' was selected for inclusion in the *Best British Short Stories 2018* anthology (Salt Publishing).

WITCHES SAIL IN EGGSHELLS

AND OTHER STORIES

CHLOE TURNER

REFLEX PRESS

First published as a collection in 2019 by Reflex Press
Abingdon, Oxfordshire, OX14 3SY
www.reflex.press

A CIP catalogue record of this book is available
from the British Library.

ISBN: 978-1-9161115-0-9

1 3 5 7 9 10 8 6 4 2

Printed and bound in Great Britain by
Clays Ltd, Elcograf S.p.A.

Front cover image by Laura Pashby
Back cover image © Constantinos / Adobe Stock

www.reflex.press/witches-sail-in-eggshells/

To my lovely Jon, thank you

CONTENTS

Hagstone

Leda lifted the necklace from the mirror's shoulder, letting the knotted stones tumble across the back of her hand. She'd thrown off last night's childish panic; had woken calm, absolved, a greedy hunger in her belly. The answer would come from the stones. She sat a moment longer, drawing the square-cut leather thong around the base of her thumb, letting one smooth pebble after another trace the lines of her palm.

But if she were looking for resolution, it would not be these dumb flints to provide it. Workhorses: so common-place on the beaches where she'd collected them, she had half a shoebox more under her bed. Enough for a half a dozen more necklaces like this one. Some were sea-polished to poor man's gemstones, but many had kept their chalky outer coat, or were warped and bulging, or pitted like skin wracked by some wretched disease. All had the hole in their heart. She rolled them in the scoop of her palm now, skim-ming their surface with her fingertips, closing her eyes to feel the voids hollowed from their cores by the sea. There was pleasure in their eroded silkiness, but no magic there.

No, the answer would lie in what was knotted into the thong alongside the fastening, so that it lay hidden under Leda's hair unless the necklace slipped or was pulled. It was the only stone she hadn't found herself: something foreign, something strange. At the surface, this lump of buffed up Mecklenburg shingle was grey-blue like many of the flints, but other colours swam beneath: strata of green, clouded patches, fleurs-de-lis of violet and brown. They shifted in Leda's memory so that the effect was subtly different every day.

With the necklace on, she liked to slide her index finger inside her collar, to feel the slippery cool of the stone against her skin. She reached there now, closed her eyes again. Smiled; yes, this was right. Walking down the stairs, hand still at her neck, she tucked the polished mass into the crook of her finger joint, better to sense its power.

*

They'd been on the beach in Dorset. She'd been twelve, thirteen maybe, but tall, so that her jeans always left a cold stripe of skin at her ankle. Her father, a vague man in baggy grey slacks, used to call her his beanpole. Her sister, Sage, *the right height for sixteen*, said that Leda's long, plimsolled feet made her look like a letter L or a small-town clown.

It was their mother—never able to sit still for long—who had suggested the sailing that afternoon, cheeks already pinking with enthusiasm and lukewarm rosé as she hustled Leda from her beach towel. There was a quiet but consistent breeze, and the next family along the estuary shore had two lightweight dinghies they were happy to lend. Leda's mother took the larger. Her outsized sunglasses flashed unknowable signals as she tacked across the channel with confidence, leaving Leda to fold herself into the cramped hull of the second boat, the boy twins from the other family along for the ride. Leda's father was elsewhere—fixing something, probably—so it was the father of the twins who launched them from the sand. Sage smirked from the picnic blanket, guarding the basket against passing dogs, she claimed.

'I don't know what I'm doing. You'll have to help.'

The boys had been staring from the far side of the boom as Leda fumbled, but now they took over the ropes, silent but not unfriendly in their relief. She sat back, trailing her fingertips through the water, glimpsing the pale blooms of jellyfish in the churn. She watched her mother's skilful passage out to the mouth of the estuary.

'What's that?' She'd noticed a string of something at the prow, mossy with petal weed.

'Hagstones,' one twin said.

'Some old rubbish,' said the other.

'Dad says they kept boats safe, in the old days.'

The first nagged at his nostril rim with a fingernail while his brother worked the tiller.

'What are they?'

'Just stones, with a hole. The sea digs it out. Or the river. Dad's always on at us to collect them.'

They were approaching the line of breakers at the river's mouth, and the water was suddenly cold. Leda retrieved her hand, tucked it into the fleece of her sleeve.

Hagstones. Adder stones. Glain Neidr. Serpent's eggs.

She started collecting them herself that summer. Brought enough home to line the windowsill, until her mother— dusting with barely contained anger, as was her way—swept them into the bin and away.

So the next summer she began again. The Gower this time. Sage, kicking sand with frustration at the lack of mobile reception, offered to help, and Leda let her, though her pleasure was in the finding. Picking her way around the sharp rocks at the river's edge, feeling the slip of weed and fin, eyes trained on the pebbles for the distinctive void at the heart of the hag. By the end of the week, the shoebox was full.

The year after, when Sage returned from a month in Germany, complete with tattoo and the lust of a Greifswald swimming instructor, she'd brought back a gift for Leda. A polished stone with a hole in its heart, tossed onto her dresser with the wrap of hashish which had spent the flight in the underside of her bra. But their mother had thrown the hash in the fire, and the argument had burned for days, so the present was forgotten, ungiven. Not long after, Sage had left again, for university in Berlin. Visiting her room from time to time, Leda lingered over the stone. Running her fingertips over its swell, even then, she'd felt its lure.

Around the same time, their father left too, though with less commotion. On the walls, photographs in which he featured gradually lessened in number, or just lost his likeness as if he had never been there at all. Afterwards, Leda and her mother stalked each other through empty rooms. Her mother's housework, ever-indignant, began to wreak casualties. Plates, of course, and whisky glasses. A Willow pattern milk jug. A chair smashed over the kitchen table. The windowsill of stones in Leda's room disappeared again one day, shipped off to the tip with any last vestiges of her father from the garage. Leda had kept silent—the gulf between them was so great now, to engage her mother would feel like defeat.

Instead, she fished the shoebox out from under her bed, leaving a bare, accusing rectangle behind in the matted dust. There had been no trips away since Sage had left, so these stones were the last of it, and she wanted them close.

Leda had already laced the rest—double knotted, as she

recalled the string on that sailing boat years back—when she remembered Sage's ungiven gift. Gathering it up that dark afternoon, she lifted it to her cheek to feel its chill. She traced the outline of her bottom lip, slipping it inside and over the wet inner places of her mouth. She might not have been the one to find it, but there was something about this stone.

From the very first day she wore the necklace, there was a shift. Tiny things: two slices of bread left of the loaf, just enough for her sandwich, and the bus rounding the corner just as she reached the stop. The old guy in her preferred seat had to stand to stretch his back. A free period after first break because Miss Vine had gone home with cramps.

Then, in the canteen queue, Alice's boyfriend, Robbie, broke away from Alice's hooked arm to ask if Leda might go over *Death of a Salesman* with him sometime. Robbie was slow, dumb as a flint himself—what did he have to offer on the American Dream? But his arms tested the seams of his suit jacket, and his lips were plumped, with only the lightest down above the upper. Leda remembered that stone against her own lip, wondered how it would feel to be pressed up against Robbie, teasing him with that delicious cool along his full mouth.

Last week she'd have made some excuse, afraid of the repercussions. But she found herself shrugging 'sure, what time?' When Alice was angry, she bit her own lower lip—thin, under her rabbity teeth—and looked uglier than she deserved.

Nothing happened with Robbie that day, though his fingers grazed her forearm as he said goodbye. But the next day, the bus was on time again—unheard of—and the woman in Leda's seat jumped up at the first stop to see to her crying child. Later, at college, Leda came first in the Spanish mocks, because Faisel—always top—was suspended for cheating. Robbie said 'alright' to her on the way out, Alice bristling a few paces behind, and his friend Pete gave him a dig in the ribs which meant something.

Walking to the bus, she heard that Rachel Harris (bane of Leda's life back at St Mark's Primary) had slipped over nothing in the canteen, breaking her nose on a table leg, just as Leda had long imagined she might. When she got home, her mother was out. There was pizza, within date, in the fridge. While she ate, she twisted the necklace's thong into a knot, so that the edge of *that* stone pinched the skin at the back of her neck.

On the third day, lifting the necklace to her throat, the stone looked darker, the clouds denser. When she fastened the knot, the thong was tight against her flesh, as if her neck had swelled overnight.

Her mother appeared in tears while Leda was eating cornflakes, spouting about neglect and regret, spilling twenty-quid notes from her purse like it was Christmas. Then, on the bus, Leda's seat came up again: the Indian guy who always carried a Bible started clutching his head before they'd even reached Park Road, getting off three stops earlier than usual. Through the bus's back window, Leda watched him grabbing for a tree trunk—one of those flimsy maples with the peeling bark—staggering like a man at sea.

Robbie was waiting at the gates, and he walked right up to campus with her, his hand in the small of her back. Later, she asked around about Alice, but people were vague, or dismissive. When Robbie invited her down Alma Road for a smoke at break, they ended up in the alleyway by the chip shop, his fat fingers probing the bent underwire of her bra.

She felt the knot in the necklace thong rolling against the brickwork as he lifted her, grunting as he did so, and the stone was warm against her neck as his lips parted the collar of her flimsy school shirt.

It might have gone further if Mr Beales hadn't walked past the end of the alleyway, and Leda hadn't got spooked and insisted they walk back to college. On the way back across the playing field, she spotted a wrap of notes in an elastic band: £100 in crisp twenties, right behind the football goal. She split it with Robbie, which brought back his stupid grin.

Then, just before the final bell, watching him dig a hole in the desk edge with a biro, came the uncompromising blast of the fire alarm. Real smoke, spilling down the sides of the design and tech building like a grey coverlet with edges you couldn't make out. Robbie stood beside her in the arts block courtyard, his big hand wrapped round hers, while students—twenty, fifty, they kept coming—fell coughing from the double doors, until the flow thinned out and the doors swung shut.

'Where's Hutton?'

'Fuck knows. He probably lit the thing.'

People around them started to look for the thin, angry man who wielded tools like weapons at the top of the DT block. He'd been Leda's tutor last year. Had taken it upon himself to remove her brand-new piercings by hand: the second stud in her lobe; the silver barbell rook through the cartilage in her upper ear; and, most painful of all, the spiral through three holes in her helix.

'Against the rules,' he'd said, each word timed to coincide with a twist of the handle, as he crushed the delicate piercings afterwards in the worktop vice.

'You don't think he's still up there?' She'd not seen Robbie worried before. The sandy freckles on the side of his neck had turned pink, and he was pinching his lip, manipulating the plump flesh.

Leda shrugged, and Robbie's eyebrows dipped in a frown of surprise. The smoke was thicker now, touchably thick, leaking from the top floor windows. Leda imagined the searing heat up there, felt the stone at her neck pulse with it. Through the archway, they heard the fire engine scream into the car park. Fire officers in bulky kit spilled across the courtyard: shouting, pointing, hoisting hoses that unrolled like giant tapeworms across the thin grass.

All around her there were hands to mouths. Girls embracing. Alice was there, on the ceramics studio steps, staring across towards Robbie like she'd seen a ghost. Stuart Mann, last to emerge, was vomiting against the backup generator. The puke was reddish: Ribena or blood. Leda didn't care. She was remembering the crack of the helix spiral, which had cost all the money she had, and £5 stolen from her mother's purse. How Mr Hutton's nostrils had flared as he held the bench with one hand and twisted the vice handle with the other. The heat was pricking sweat across her forehead.

Staff were hustling the crowd back now. Leda resisted, wanting to see.

'Out the front, main drive. The fire brigade need this space now.' All cleavage and tie-dye, Mrs Barratt was swollen with sudden importance.

It was Robbie who led Leda away, her eyes still trained on the double doors at the foot of the building. At her neck, the stone was scorching. She rubbed under her collar, expecting her flesh to be sticky with burn, but there was nothing. She didn't have to look at the stone to know that the clouds inside it would have darkened to black.

Guilt did come, but only when the body was disgorged from the staircase on a stretcher forced through the double doors, a fire officer at head and foot. Hutton was covered, but his face was exposed.

'He's alright, then,' Robbie said, fist pumping.

'Alive, anyway.'

At last, remorse. It seemed to ooze from the other stones at her neck, seeping across her clavicles, down her sternum, fanning across her ribs. With its whooping siren, an ambulance took the corner at pace.

'Come back to mine,' Robbie said. 'This stuff, I can't explain it. It's made me feel horny.'

His hand was on her waistband, bitten down fingers already pinging the elastic of her tights. But she wriggled away, easing the necklace's thong from the skin of her neck at the same time. She wanted to be free of them both.

'No,' she said, and 'Mum needs me at home,' remembering the tears and cash disgorged at the breakfast table.

'Suit yourself,' Robbie shrugged, but the fabric around his biceps tightened, and he didn't smile as he turned away.

Leda started down the drive, a screw of fear in her belly. She'd give the bus a miss tonight. She needed fresh air and somewhere to dump this thing. She'd walk the park route; all sorts got chucked in that lake. But as she was passing the stop, the bus pulled up alongside her. And when she ignored it, the driver tooted and waved, so she felt like she had no choice. *Her* seat was free, of course, though every other one was taken, and a man in a suit was slumping on a hand-pull just inside the rear door. She pulled her knees together, closed her eyes.

At the other end, Leda planned to sling the necklace in the skip outside Number 32, but there was no sign of the huge yellow carton which had sat there for months. She would have thrown it in the wheelie bin at home, but her mother was already there on the doorstep, ushering her in. She was wearing the daisy dress Leda's dad used to love, and the tears had been replaced with a smile that almost reached her eyes.

The first chance she got, Leda ran to her room, catching the waxy flesh of her neck in the three mirrors of her dressing table as she yanked the thong away from her skin. The knot was reluctant to give. When she'd worked it loose at last, there were red marks where the stones had been, and a pinpoint of stiffness at the back of her neck.

In her palm, the stone was dull now, the clouds close-set and surly. She thought of Hutton: the blackened flesh around his hairline, the limp way his arm had begun to slip from the side of the stretcher before the medic tucked it away. Bile surged in her throat, and her breath felt shallow and unreliable. *It couldn't have been, surely?* She was tired suddenly, spent. *Could it?* But the tiredness, it was seeping up under her eyelids, weighting them, blurring her thoughts so that she could only think of sleep. The morning, then. She'd unlace the stones, walk the park way, throw the lot of them into the depths of the pond. Burn the thong on the caretaker's bonfire, if that's what it took. But tomorrow...

She didn't make it under the duvet, and as she slipped towards sleep fully clothed, she dreamed of a hand moving through oil-dark water. Of cellophane jellyfish. Of glowing stones sinking through the grimy depths. At the foot of her bed, the necklace lay draped across the dressing table where she had left it, reflected in all three mirrors so that the sodium glow filtering through the curtains from the street seemed to collect upon it. The hagstone waited.

Piñata

Ten minutes before the first guest is due, Marlie Harris is drawing. The birthday girl's trainers dangle over the sofa edge, their sequinned sides pulsing with the rotation of the glitter ball. She's got a sketchbook on her lap, but with a pink triangle of tongue pressed between thin lips, she's tracing an outline across the inside of the left-hand armrest instead. Penis and scrotal sack, in black marker pen, disquieting against the crinkled cream leather.

The drawing is careful and, for an eight-year-old, admirably correct in its anatomy. It'll be something she's recalled from the inside covers of her cousin Kieron's school books. Marlie is always keen to demonstrate what she's learnt from Kieron. Last time he visited from Dublin, he mocked her rainbow doodles. (And for owning a doll at eight years old... Astrid was buried the next day, with little ceremony, at the cat-shit end of the sandpit.)

A refined nose might pick up a hint of juniper in the air. Marlie's mother, Lou, is in the kitchen, pouring a generous Bombay Sapphire: several hours before her usual tipple, and light on the tonic. But aside from the gin's astringent ping, the overriding odour is of candy floss. Hot pink candy. The atmosphere is thickening with the sweet stink of it.

'Christ, Stu, how much did you put in that thing? It

reeks.' Clacking through to the lounge in heels she's already regretting, Lou glares at the machine on the sideboard. A gleaming apparatus of industrial proportions, the machine whickers flesh coloured sugar grains into soft, pink clouds. Lou slops gin onto polished maple in her haste to access the off switch. She can't find it; twists a dial which eases the machine's speed instead, then crouches to gather up the pink fluff which has fallen.

'Oof,' she says, then remembers Stu pursing his lips, saying that noise makes her sound like some knackered old bag. Her heels buckle outwards as she heaves herself back upright, grabbing the sofa back for support. Who's he to talk? He's got grey curls in his chest hair, and a sag around his jaw. Lou throws the handful of candy floss back into the metal pan, feels the tacky sugar residue in her palm.

Terri-Ann Davies came up with the candy floss maker, from the sweet shop where she works. It's the only reason her daughter Joanne will attend the party today. The urge to avoid—exclude—Joanne, with her ratty plait and her charity shop Disney dresses, is one of a bare handful of sentiments that mother and daughter share, though for different reasons. Lou doesn't feel good about it, but candy floss makers don't come cheap, and Marlie Harris is in the habit of drawing up a long list of birthday demands.

'Marlie, tell me next time, yeah? If it's overflowing,' Lou says, careful to keep it light. 'Now, where are those skewers I bought?'

Marlie doesn't reply, just eases a scatter cushion from under her side so that the marker pen outline is better concealed under its purple silk piping. It'll stay covered for a while yet.

Even with the dial turned down, the sideboard is rocking

with the vigour of the candy-floss maker's spin. With each fresh batch of spun sugar, the aluminium box judders forward a centimetre or two. But Lou has already moved on to the lid of the underused piano. She rearranges the food that she set up earlier, shifting paper plates of cocktail sausages and crisps. Looks behind the pot of hummus that her sister, Han, recommended as a token gesture, and under the tray of crudités she knows will be ignored.

'What's this, what's this? Did I hear there was candy floss in the house? As if by magic?' Marlie's father, Stuart, is halfway down the stairs. His whole body swings one way and then the other with each step, a mobile swagger which he's adopted to fit the lower centre of gravity of middle age. He's slicked back his hair today because he likes to think he's still got it.

'It's not magic, Dad. It's a metal thing that whizzes round. And you bought the sugar, anyway, so you know that.'

Marlie may be rolling her eyes, but she still jumps up and runs to hug her father, catching him at the foot of the stairs. She fans newly polished rainbow fingernails over the midnight blue polyester of his Everton shirt.

'You got me, baby girl. Now, is my princess all ready for her special day?'

Marlie steps back, gathering up the flounced red tulle of her pageant dress, and curtsies for her Daddy. The hairdresser wired her ponytails earlier, so they stick out at right angles above her ears. It doesn't look as elegant as she'd hoped. When Stuart grins so that his two front teeth hug his lower lip, Lou hears her sister, Han's, voice, begging her to drag him to the dentist. But if Han knew him better, she'd know that his paralysing fear of the drill trumps his vanity; he'd have done it long ago if he could.

'Wait a minute. Which wicked witch has put a blemish on my beautiful princess? I must break this spell at once.'

'What is it, Dad?'

When Marlie sat back earlier to admire the detail of her drawing, she caught the apple of her right cheek with the pen, and it's this streak that Stuart has spotted. He licks the pad of his thumb, smooths it across the mark. Then, frowning, rubs harder.

'What you got here, love? It won't come off.'

Lou's shaking her head. 'Five minutes to go. Could we please...?' She promised herself she wouldn't lose it.

'Keep your hair on, Lou-Lou. Just give us some of that stuff you use. If there's any left, the way you slap it on.'

Lou's shoulders stiffen, but she's turned for the stairs when the doorbell goes. *Happy Birthday!* Stu likes her to change the chime each week between the six available. Her preference, though she couldn't name it, is Beethoven's Fifth. Increasingly, she hates them all. Today's was a given.

Marlie's crying now, snorting like a piglet at the trough. It's not just the pen mark. The glitter she glued to her forehead has begun to irritate her skin, turning it patchy and red, exaggerating the pink of her eyes.

'Tell them to go, Dad.'

'Baby girl, it's just a tiny dot. I should've never mentioned it.'

The doorbell chimes on, and shapes shift in the frosted glass of the frame. It looks like a crowd. And there's a yellow blob above them, squeaking against the glass.

Lou comes back down the stairs with a concealer tube, and Stuart glances over. She can't meet his eye, adjusting the green rayon ruffles around her neckline. He hates the top, she knows it. She wasn't sure, but Han sent the link to the online store. *Those stuck-up bitches from the Edge End Estate won't be able to touch you in this.* The elastic's already pinching at her waist where it meets the soft skin of her stomach, probably leaving a mark all round. She must remember not to lift her arms above her head.

The yellow shape squeaks again, and a small hand hammers the glass. It'll be those stuck-up bitches now. She wishes Han wasn't on the other side of the Irish Sea. Just like them to be early for a nosey. And bringing their own balloon, for Christ's sake, as if she might not provide enough.

Stuart snatches the concealer, dabs an untidy blob of mismatched colour onto his daughter's cheek. That done, he reaches to stroke a plait, then thinks better of it.

'Come on, love, you look like a proper princess. And all your princes are hammering that door down, wanting to treat you like a lady.'

'Everything's ruined. I won't be pretty. Mum can't even make candy floss properly. And I hate the piñata. It doesn't look like Elsa's dress. It looks like a big, blue poo.'

Stuart raises an eyebrow at Lou. 'I did say get the one in Asda.'

'It was supposed to be a treat, making it together. I...'

Stuart snorts, and she gives up.

'Certainly took long enough. Next time let's just get the proper one, yeah, and miss out the weeks of glue and shit all over the living room,' he says.

Lou stares at him until he lifts his shoulders in a shrug.

'Get the door, would you?'

She doesn't, retreating to the kitchen instead. The gin is waiting for her. In its pretty pale blue bottle, it reminds her of sea glass on a beach; of steeply banked sand down to white ribbon waves. She pours another two fingers into a tall glass.

Back in the lounge, Marlie's still crying, but she's spotted her reflection in the mirror on the far wall. She pouts with each sob until gradually she is just pouting.

'Right, baby girl. You all set? Are we letting these reprob... retrobate... whatever, in, or what? You know I'll send them all home if you want me to, but they might have presents...'

Stu reaches for Marlie's armpit. She squirms away from the tickle, feigning irritation, but he's worked his magic.

'Okay, then,' she says, heavy emphasis on the 'kay'.

There's a moment of silence between the doorbell's final peal and Stuart turning the latch. Then—freeze-frame—the children are revealed, stoppered into the doorway in their desperation to be first. The three women behind lean inwards: one with a package in rose-gold tissue, one in a cloud of Chanel Cristalle, one on a mobile phone.

It's Robbie Wainwright who breaks the seal, elbowing his way into the hall, his bowtie elastic already stretched so that it sags below his collar. Tegan and Mitzy are close behind, mobbing Marlie in a screaming, whirling confusion of ripped gilt wrap and flammable fabrics. Stuart steps aside, arms lifted theatrically, the grin of a clown, as the rest of the kids surge in. There's a shout from the gate as he's leaning back to close the door.

'Sorry, mate.' Stu's friend Andy with his daughter Georgia. They cross the threshold just as Lou returns, smile painted on and a mouthful of botanicals. By the standards of Stuart's football mates, Andy is as well-behaved as he is well-groomed. Today, his hair is so thickly waxed that light rain has settled along the spikes in perfect droplets, and he's wearing a collared shirt like the one Stuart refused. She's oblivious to the obscene tattoo which sits just under its collar.

'Know what it's like if that's any consolation,' Andy goes on, his voice so low, it's a growl. 'These parties, wild! They did over our place last week—she was gutted Marlie was sick, Georgia was—but truth be known I was grateful to have one less.'

'Don't worry, mate. The wife told me. Got your brother in redecorating the staircase, she said, where the little fuckers took the plaster out.'

A passing child hears the profanity, giggles. Lou winces as the two men congratulate each other with back slaps and a half hug. At least the three wise women won't have heard; they're too busy casing the room. Divided for better coverage, they're poking manicured fingernails, taking in the Primark prints and Stu's vast telly, and the six-inch plastic flamenco dancer he brought her back from Marbella that time, which Lou's forgotten to hide.

She glances over at the new sofa, hoping they notice that, at least. It cost enough. It was that or an extension to the side return, and she took a chance that the sofa would get more attention. Worth it, surely, even if Stuart's still whingeing about worktop space for his deep fat fryer. But the women show no interest in the sofa, and even though Lou left a line of shoes in the porch as a hint, Robbie's already planted his size three Nike Airs on the middle cushion. For a moment it looks like he might kick the scatter cushion off the drawing, but then he's over the end and down, knocking Mitzy sideways. The candy floss machine shudders another millimetre towards the edge.

The children have proliferated to every corner now, squeezing under furniture on some impromptu treasure hunt. Tegan, the smart alec whose mother, Veronica, runs an insurance company, is unwinding a cloud of candy floss, looping it across her shoulders like a sugary boa. Lou retrieves a plate of sausages from the floor, leaving the chipolata that's the smeared casualty of someone's heel, and looks away from the spilt squash over the piano lid. She forces a smile, so at least Stuart can't complain she's got that ugly fussing look on, and takes a long draught of Sapphire. The tang of the tonic bubbles sears up through her adenoids.

Happy Birthday! The doorbell starts up again. More children, and behind them comes the entertainer, drab and underwhelming in a tatty velvet smock and jester's hat. This was Veronica's recommendation, and Lou wonders if she's been set up. The woman backs herself into a corner, blocking off children with the vast disco speakers Stu borrowed from a man down The Bull and Bear, and starts filling modelling balloons. Every time she twists the rubber, it squeaks like nails on a blackboard, and Lou's grateful when someone turns the music on full blast.

Katy Perry's 'Roar'. The girls take their squealing up another notch, and Robbie grinds his pelvis to the beat. His mother juts out her lower lip as the other mothers point but still takes a photo on her phone. On the far side of the room, Stuart starts to copy the boy. It's repellent, but at least three of the mothers clap along. By the time he's moved on to Taylor Swift's 'Shake It Off', no one's watching Robbie anymore, so the boy starts to kick the piano leg. Veronica is miming a passable striptease, and Stu's miming to Andy that he should film her doing it.

Happy Birthday! The chimes clash with Swift, and this time it's Joanne, standing alone on the path. As Louise walks towards her, Terri-Ann waves from the car window beyond the gate, then her knackered old Punto is away. Louise grits her teeth. It's a worse dress than last year: orange skirt with black spiders, one legless. The whole ensemble clearly meant for Hallowe'en, but it's June. The girl's hair's not been brushed. The gift she's carrying looks thin and small.

But then, like a slug in the gut, Lou remembers Terri-Ann back at school.

All those times, they come rushing back as one. Being ushered into the classroom that first day, the ranks of alien, suspicious faces, the sweet relief of Terri's grin from the far side, pointing to the spare seat beside her. That night on the common in year nine, when those boys wouldn't let them go home: pushing them on the swings—gently first, then much too high—twisting the cables so they were trapped in the swing seats. Boys' hands everywhere, and Lou'd gone mute, so it was left to Terri to scream for help from the man in the ice-cream van. And then Terri's face, tight from the effort of not crying, when Stuart finally blurted out that he'd been seeing someone else, and that someone was Lou.

She takes the gift from the girl now, slips it into her pocket—best Marlie and the rest don't have the chance to rip the wrapper off. It occurs to Lou she could sneak Joanne round the back now. Make an excuse, get her into something from Marlie's packed rails. She takes the girl's hand, but Stuart's on the step: 'Ah...' rolling his eyes, 'again.'

It's too late, and anyway, the urge has gone. Joanne will be alright. These kids aren't like those kids, and it was all a long time ago. She lets go of Joanne's hand, but the girl doesn't move, paralysed by the wall of sound. Lou has to usher her in with her palm against the prickly fabric of the dress.

Inside, someone has pulled back the curtains and the glitter ball's manic: light beads duck and dive over the Artex. The girls are wrestling on the sofa, shifting the scatter cushion so that one half of a ball sack has slipped into view, though no one's noticed it yet. Robbie's skidding on the rug. Stuart's in the middle of it all, with a bottle of Rioja in one hand and his novelty opener in the other. Mitzy's mother, Emmie, has got her hand round Sir Perky's appendage and she's giggling, her lower lip coral pink and loose. When Stu gives her the glass, she takes the first sip without taking her eyes off him. Louise wonders how it would be not to care.

There's a shriek then. Georgia's collided with Emmie's yellow heel, and red wine is sloshed across the faux ash linoleum. The girl's alright, but Emmie's sleeveless top is a Rioja leopard print.

'I'll go,' says Stu, and Emmie goes after him, exhaling through her nose in little gasps as she pats uselessly at the white silk of her vest. They don't come back. Lou gets on her knees, uses a tissue that someone hands her to mop up the worst of it. Closes her eyes and thinks of that beach. Of chalky, smooth pebbles that she could hurl into the waves.

'What the...?' she hears, as she stands up at last, white stars in the corners of her vision like when she stands too quickly in the bath. Veronica's got the cushion in her hand. A new network of tight lines has appeared between the edge of her nostrils and her upper lip as if the puppet master is pulling tendons from within. It's not her house, who gives her the right?

'It was Joanne,' says the first child, before Veronica's even got her Rouge Essentiel nail extended towards the life-sized cock on the sofa arm. Louise almost laughs. The drawing's no worse than she could have done herself.

'I saw her,' says Robbie's mum, though she's barely lifted her eyes from her phone since she's arrived.

Georgia's recovered from her collision long enough to get hold of Joanne, and she shoves her forward. Other voices chime in. Robbie sticks his foot out automatically, but Joanne steps over it, eyes down. At least one woman mutters something about 'dirty' and 'Hallowe'en'. Lou feels as if her feet are not on stable ground.

Someone's turned the music off, so everyone hears the laugh from the kitchen. Lou knows Joanne didn't draw on the sofa arm. Even if Marlie didn't have that face on—her mouth is turned down in a full arc of defiance and one eyebrow ever so slightly lifted—she'd know who the culprit was. One day she will confront the fact that she doesn't really like her daughter, but today is not the day.

She looks around. Sees the jury have given their verdict. Perhaps it is too late to intervene, in any case.

'Joanne, I'm calling your mother,' Lou says gently.

Joanne holds herself very still. There's a hole in her right sock, and through it they can see the toenail on her big toe has been untended so long, it's started to curve up and away from the skin.

'She won't have it on her. She's got no credit.' Joanne looks at her feet as she says it. Why doesn't she deny it? Marlie would have denied it immediately before she knew what she'd been accused of.

Veronica snorts, strokes the deep red of a fingernail with the thumb of the other hand. 'Dirty little thing. Just take her home. I would.'

'Mum's at work.'

Joanne doesn't cry. The only sign of her distress is a tremor at her shoulder, where a legless spider clings on to the tattered remnants of a web.

'Take her there, then. It's a party. You're not running a crèche,' Veronica says.

Lou takes a deep breath. Tegan's mother is the playground's undisputed queen. A bad word from Veronica and every school run will be a misery. Lou quashes inconvenient memories of Terri-Ann: tiny saves and kindnesses. She looks away from Joanne's wrists, so thin that the lump at her wrist where the ulna meets the tessellated bones of the hand, stands proud like a tumour. She'll make it up to the girl. The party is over for her now, anyway.

'Stu can do it. I'll get him now.'

Veronica nods at her, satisfied. Steps past Joanne as if she were something unspeakable on the rug. Presses play on the stereo—only the tiniest frown at the outdated model—so Taylor Swift comes blasting back into the room. Andy moves in for a closer look at the drawing, looks about for Stu, padded cheeks sagging when his friend's not about to share the joke. The candy floss machine rattles, empty of sugar, hanging proud of the sideboard's edge.

When Lou comes into the kitchen, she doesn't realise at first what she's seeing. Mitzy's mother is facing away, towards the window that looks out over the garden, and Stu is right behind her, leaning past her with his hand on the tap. But the water's not running, and he's close to her, too close, so that his groin must be pressed hard against the back pockets of Emmie's skinny jeans.

Lou starts to wheel about, catching her hip on the hard plastic edge of Stu's fryer, sending a bolt of pain up through her ribs.

'I told you, we should have done the side return,' Stu doesn't say because he can't speak. He's looking round at Lou now, but his face has turned a dull terracotta shade she recognises. Lou's surprised by how bored it makes her feel this time, how the sight of his belly peeling away from Emmie's fragile vest makes her nauseous rather than jealous. She doesn't make eye-contact with Emmie. Can't be bothered. It's not about her.

'Wait, Lou...' she hears, as she retraces her steps, but she doesn't turn. When she gets to the lounge, Joanne is still on the rug, alone. A loosely anchored skiff in a storm. Robbie and the other boys bounce around her to One Direction.

'Can you turn it down?' Lou shouts across the room. Andy nods, mouthing something back, twisting the dial the wrong way. The light beads from the glitter ball judder in their path around the walls with the bass. The children's eyes are wild. Robbie is break dancing in a pool of squash between the piano legs.

'I can't...' Lou shouts.

People are looking. Her cheeks must be as flaming as they feel. For a moment the faces are like masks in a play, shifting and gurning across her vision. Then comes the mechanical thud, and the scream that follows it. The candy floss machine has been driven over the edge by the incessant bass, and someone has broken its fall. Identical dents have been left in Georgia's leg and on the waxy surface of the lino. She's lying white-faced, staring at the unnatural depression the machine has left in the bony core of her shin.

'Let's have that off. Mate, I'll get the ambulance.' Stu's there at once, shouting across the noisy room. He flicks the switch on the stereo, his hand grazing Andy's shoulder as his friend bends over his daughter. Lou realises she's been frozen, staring.

'I'll make the call,' she says, grateful to be relieved of the sight of that leg.

In the frantic minutes that follow, Georgia starts up a low moan, and a couple of other children begin to cry. Joanne doesn't move from the rug. Robbie picks up sausages from the floor, tucking them under his lips to make fat vampire teeth.

'Tegan, baby, we should go.' Veronica is wiping her hands with a disinfectant wipe she's pulled from her handbag. Her daughter whines and pulls on her arm. Veronica brushes her off with the wipe.

'But we haven't done the piñata.' Marlie's outraged squeal combines with Georgia's moan and Tegan's whine in a dreadful choir of complaint.

'Quickly then, while we wait for the ambulance.' Stu's recovered himself. Like a child, his guilt is short-lived and quickly turns to indignant denial. Nothing cheers him more than a crisis. He lifts the blue papier mâché shape from on top of the bookshelf, sets it down on a bare patch of floor. The glitter ball's light beads still spin pointlessly around the walls, illuminating the crushed food and spillages.

'Ewww,' says a child's voice.

'Make sure you give Georgia enough space.'

'Some party,' Lou hears behind her. This'll be playground fuel for weeks.

Stu hands the toy baseball bat to Marlie for the first strike, but she misses the piñata altogether, leaving a dent in the coffee table leg that is an unwanted reminder of the groaning girl in the corner. Marlie strikes again, and again, but the bat falls weakly away from the papier mâché core.

'You made it too hard, Mum.' Her arms are folded. She is rigid with disgust. Robbie snatches the bat before she can throw it aside.

'I'll do it. You watch.'

His face reddens as if a dial is being turned inside, and the mould does give a little under his barrage of abuse, but it doesn't yield. A few others try. Mitzy kicks the piñata with the toe of a glittery shoe. The lacy trim around Elsa's dress comes away, so the Disney princess looks as shameful as Lou feels.

All at once, impatience and overtired laughter bloom in the group around Lou, and then there is a move as one towards the door. The sharks have had their fill. It is time. The three wise women exit quickly, leaving a lingering trace of Chanel and a tide of guilt. Robbie kicks the doorframe as he passes, still griping for another go with the bat. Too late, Lou realises that she's forgotten the party bags, which sit upstairs in accusing ranks across her bedroom floor. She thinks of the charm bracelets and watches, in multiples that she could not afford, and wonders if the market stall might take them back.

Soon after, the ambulance arrives: two booted men in high-vis march in, grinding the last of the food between the cracks in the lino tiles. With a tiny twitch of his head, one gestures at the sofa arm, raising his eyebrows to his mate as they lift the girl onto the stretcher. Georgia's smiling weakly now, already contemplating lucrative weeks of convalescence. Stu claps Andy on the back as he follows the ambulance men down the path.

'Sorry, mate.'

'Not your fault.'

Stu wanders out with his friend to see the ambulance off.

At last, it is only Lou, Marlie and Joanne. Around them, the full scale of the destruction is revealed. The sofa cushion lies in a sodden mass of molten candy floss. The uplifted arm of the plastic flamenco dancer has been wrapped around its throat in a stranglehold. Bare of its shielding cushion, the sofa arm's obscene inner cheek is in full view. The fingers of a chocolate handprint are clearly visible on the other arm.

'You ruined my party, Mum.' Marlie is already stomping upstairs. Any minute now she will pass the open bedroom door, pumping the bellows of her fury at the sight of the forgotten party bags.

Joanne still has not moved. Someone has pulled the witch's cauldron from the belt of her dress, and her hair has come loose from its plait. Lou wants to say sorry, but she can't find the words. She reaches for the baseball bat, which has rolled under the coffee table next to a discarded shoe, and hands it to Joanne. She hears the wail from upstairs, and Joanne's face is a question. Lou shakes her head and points to the piñata.

Joanne makes the first strike, and then Lou joins her, grabbing the Velux window pole from the corner, which thuds into the piñata's casing again and again with a satisfying smash. The green of Lou's shirt darkens at the armpits, but they keep up the battery. At last a tiny tear appears in the papier mâché bodice. A tear that eases open into a wide rip, and further still so that the piñata yawns to reveal the sweet wrappers inside. Lou takes a handful, passes them to Joanne, motions for the girl to sit. Then she picks up the pole again, twisting it for the best grip, and returns to the sickly iced-blue shell of the piñata.

'What you doing, Lou? Think the woman's lost it,' she

hears from the doorway. But it's too late by then; her face is burning with the pleasure of it. With every strike of the pole, the void inside Elsa's dress gapes more widely. The sweets are pulverised in their jewelled wrappings. As she pummels the bloated mass of the thing, she thinks about Marlie. About her daughter's sour little face, and the eye roll she has inherited from her father. She thinks about Emmie, how her thin hand with its opal rings covered Stuart's fat palm on her thigh. She thinks about Robbie, with his random acts of destruction, and whether she could call herself any better than him now, smashing this piñata as if it had done her some wrong. And she thinks about Joanne, how the girl's face did not alter as she was wrongly accused, so used to being let down. About Terri-Ann, and all those times.

'Let's go,' Lou says at last, laying down the pole and taking Joanne's hand.

'What the...?' Stu says, as she pushes past him in the doorway, but the cool air outside strengthens her resolve.

Joanne's hand, sticky in her palm, feels as fragile as the skeleton of a mouse. There's no sign of the Punto, but it's not far to Terri-Ann's.

'There's something I need to say to your mother,' Lou says, as they walk together down the path.

Inches Apart

Ben was only supposed to be paying the bill, but he never came back to the bedroom, and there was no sign of him now as Rachel strolled through the public areas of the hotel, forcing herself to keep smiling. No sign of *him*. No sign of *her*. The whole, empty, frost-white expanse of the nine-hole pitch-and-putt course was visible from the drawing-room windows, and he wouldn't have had time to make it down to the lake. Rachel could go to the room to wait, but that would be worse. Instead, she slipped out through the front door, crunching over frozen lawns, to the side of the hotel and then the back. Ben wouldn't be here either, of course, amongst the fire escapes and wire food crates and weeds growing through concrete, but she'd give him the benefit of the doubt.

It took some time to walk the length of the back wall, picking her way through the detritus of the hotel's industrial backside. At the far end, a sheet of render had slipped from the masonry like sloughed skin, and frost crystals had collected along the sheared edge. Stepping round it and turning the corner, Rachel found herself beside the black tarpaulin of the hotel's outdoor swimming pool. It had seen better days; she'd forgotten it was even here. The ladder was buckled on one side, rusty, and blooming with frost flowers even where the chrome remained. The cover over the pool's surface was bleached and stained.

She stepped closer now, tiptoeing around the striped aqua tiles that framed the pool, pausing in front of a leaf net and—tipped from it before it had been dropped—a collection of dead things. Disgusted but drawn, she sifted this frozen flotsam with the toe of her boot. Frosted lumps that might have been wasps. Butterfly wings, grey and shapeless like newspaper left in the rain. Something too long to be a mouse, its body barely thicker than its tail now, with the fur frozen to its skin. She pulled her coat closer, exhaled twin streams of steam. There was a smell of mildew, and cat shit, and something wrong: perhaps it was that furred creature, whatever it was, as it warmed in the pale glow of the winter sun.

Rachel stamped her feet. She was about to walk on when she noticed the pool's cover had been pulled back at one corner. Underneath, a layer of waxy, opaque ice had clogged white around the legs of the ladder. Green beneath: deep green. Then, leaning over, frost snapping at her palm as she gripped the ladder's curve, Rachel saw there was something there. In the ice. Two solids, each the size of a hand. She crouched, waiting for her eyes to adjust to the shadow of the tarp. The edges resolved themselves into an outline of spines, of pointed noses, clawed feet. Two hedgehogs, inches apart and head to head: frozen. She imagined a cuboid cut from the ice with a saw; those two creatures, in freeze frame. Ploughing the solidifying water at the moment of death, their soft undersides as fur-sodden and limp as the butterflies' wings.

Nauseated, she turned away. They'd visited the hotel once before, her and Ben, but it had been late spring then. Too cold for the pool still, but she had a memory of the water as blue-clean, nothing like this place of death. Ben had been at his fulsome best that weekend, charming everyone. Holding her hand as they waited to check in. The hotel manager, a wiry man with one broken eye, had taken a fancy to them at once—to Ben, anyway—treating them in his dated way, with complimentary sherries, and a table saved near the congealing trays of the breakfast buffet.

Rachel had found the hotel odd, old-fashioned. Ben had liked it, and they were not long married, so it was enough to be together. She remembered walking through fields of fattening lambs, and further, to the edge of a reservoir that was belted with the hooped arches of a brick-built dam, like something from a film. They'd climbed alongside streams thick with huge pebbles. His hand had rarely left the small of her back. Once, they'd made love on a wooded hillside, amongst bruised daffodil stalks and the white stars of the wood anemone.

This time, arriving late and crabby, they'd stood a little apart as they waited at the reception desk. Waiting for the paperwork to be completed, she'd looked up to find Ben staring at a woman on a sofa in the hall.

'Busted,' he'd said, laughing, when he realised he'd been caught out. It was what he said about women in magazines—they were both allowed one free pass, he'd announced too early in the marriage—but he'd never said it about flesh and blood before.

The woman had been all in black, something big and gold around her neck, and the man she'd been with had seemed older, withdrawn. Later, in the bar, she'd been there again. It had been Rachel who'd suggested going down early, thinking they'd have a cocktail before dinner, remembering too late that the menu didn't stretch to that. The woman had been alone this time. Her husband had been called away on urgent business, she'd said.

'Don't I look silly,' the woman had said. It was a special occasion, and now, alone for the evening, she complained of feeling overdressed. Rachel had watched Ben watch the woman smooth the silky fabric of an evening dress over the gentle curve of her waist; had felt the pinch of her own trousers. Pregnancy had made Rachel fat, but not because she had a baby inside her. Clomid and gonadotrophins, agonists and antagonists, tablets and jabs and gels: a seething mass of drugs that had clogged her system for months. She'd pushed around the cubes of ice in the gin she shouldn't be drinking, reminding her for a moment of the single, frozen embryo which might represent their last chance.

Rachel came to the last corner now, which took her back round to the front of the hotel. They should never have come. This wasn't a place well-suited to winter. Even under the frost, the minigolf course had been thick with leaves when they'd crossed it yesterday, and they'd found the boating lake frozen solid, a lump of dead feathers on the muddied edge. Deep potholes marred the tarmac, and rooks had congregated in accusing gangs in the tall trees which lined the car park. The hotel's roof was patched around one chimney with a sheet of pink plastic.

It was Ben who'd asked the woman to join them for dinner last night, touching her arm as he did so, fingers tracing the skin just above the swirling cuff which cupped the flesh of her upper arm. Rachel had expected him to apologise later when they were briefly alone—it was their last night, why could the woman not eat in her room if she preferred not to dine at a table for one?—but he'd shrugged when she'd complained. Up close, the woman had been a little older than Rachel had realised, the finest lace ladder running up from the hollow of her neck. She'd talked easily, throwing back Merlot in greedy gulps. Told wild stories of an international life.

Much later, Rachel had woken in darkness to find the bed shaking; soft, urgent, animal noises coming from the far side. Ben had said he wasn't in the mood when they were undressing, as happened so often these days. They'd both shuddered as the rhythm of his hand reached its peak.

The car park was busy now: idling taxis crisscrossed the potholes, and a coach with steamed-up windows disgorged a fill of Japanese women in thin dresses. There was no sign of Ben. Rachel walked amongst the cars, stepping on ridges of frozen mud at the car park's edge. Then suddenly, there he was, loading matching luggage into the boot of a taxi on the far side. In her mind, Rachel had built the woman up into a cartoon Cruella de Vil, but it was worse than that. She was softer, slinkier. More real. Her lips were subtly drawn. Her fur coat was a rich brown, its pelt grazing her mid-thigh. Bare above heeled boots, she had the legs of a much younger woman. Even in the depths of that coat, her curves showed through, and her luminous skin was pink-cheeked in the cold.

Rachel watched the woman shake Ben's hand and then hold it a moment; there was intimacy there. The palm of her other was on his chest. Perhaps a finger slipped between the buttons of the cotton placket to the cooling skin beneath his shirt. The hotel manager looked on from the steps, smiling.

Ben seemed to sense Rachel's presence then, and he turned and waved. He was smiling, and a stranger would have thought nothing of it, but even from here she could see the duck and rise of his Adam's apple as he swallowed hard. The woman lifted a hand to no one in particular and slipped inside the cab. Bare flesh swivelled on the seat, skirt inching up a fraction, as she closed the door. The taxi left at once, brake lights pulsing only briefly as it swung down under the railway bridge and away.

Rachel knew there would be a moment that night when Ben would go to the bathroom, his set-aside clothes laid out on the bed like a flat-packed man. She would be able to check the pockets if she wanted, and she knew there'd be something there. A stray bead from that gilt choker, perhaps, kept as a keepsake, or a smudge, dark as blood, on the white cotton of his collar. A number written in his messy scrawl on a corner of the hotel's postcard. Perhaps a single hair, not Rachel's blonde, left entangled in his wool blazer's lapel. It was whether she chose to see it.

Rachel thought again of the hedgehogs in the swimming pool, of those creatures lifted in a chunk of ice, like flies caught in amber, clawing towards each other in the solidifying cold. A frozen tussle, two boars wrestling even as the water turned their blood to ice, or was it something else? A male and a female? Two warm bodies scrabbling for each other, seeking something—rescue, comfort, death-defying sex—as darkness closed around them. When the chance came that night, she wondered what choice she would make.

Labour of Love

First, for the back of the bed, a row of puckered yellow corn: Honeydew, for its sweetness. She dibbed neat holes in the earth, feeling the sand crackle under her thumbnail as she pushed down into the organic crumb. A parallel drill of cannellini: perfect white beans, a shallow handful from the bowl. As she knelt, loose stones made themselves comfortable in the soft tissue of her knees. The final row was for squash: three creamy seeds for each hollow in the soil. Fairy tokens, light as air. The strongest seedling would race to colonise the front of the bed, creeping between the stems of the other plants, spilling its heart-shaped vine down amongst the gravel.

Three Sisters, they called it, Three Sisters planting. Corn and bean and squash, lying top to toe. She thought of her own siblings, so close and now so far away: her sister, minding a bookshop beside a lake in Ohio, and her brother in Kabul, with a wife who used to love him, and a job that threatened his life every day. And she thought of the baby inside her, barely there at all. No siblings for him; she felt too old now. So who would grow and thrive alongside him, this strange little seedling, whom she had never expected to come at all?

As a child, she'd assumed she would marry, of course, and

that children of her own would come. That she'd help pull on contrary wellies, wave off school trips, lay her own slippers beside another, larger pair. But the owner of that pair never materialised or didn't hang around, more like. A chance encounter at a trade show when the snow was still on the ground. When seeds had been selected, and new tools picked from the shiny racks, she'd gone for drinks in town, a few beers by the fire in The Ship. He'd been in Taunton for a conference at the Manor, had struck up conversation while they stood at the bar. An American—they'd talked about the almond fields in Fresno, the yellow mustard that carpets the vineyards of Monterey County every spring, and the pleasure to be found in watching things grow. She'd liked him, although his hands seemed small and sickly next to her weather-hardened paws, and he'd uttered small sounds that had made her fear she'd hurt him. She'd toasted her own bread in the morning, but he'd already left when she came back with the tray.

That taste in her mouth was back now, metallic like the silty clay of the Levels. It had come on almost at once, so she'd barely needed the plastic pen with its chromatogram window and its cheery leaflet to confirm the news. Though the taste faded a little sooner after waking each day, along with the sickness. *Your baby is as big as a blueberry*, said the book her sister sent. The waistband of her jeans already pinched as she knelt over the soil. It wouldn't be long before she too began to swell and grow.

Weeks later, it seemed unlikely that those jeans had ever fitted. She took to wearing an old canvas skirt tied at the back with a bow, and the tunic tops she'd favoured back at art college. Only a couple had survived the moths, and they faded to the colour of soil as summer wore on. When they became too tatty at last, she cut them for cloths and drove into town for saggy black dresses which expanded as she did. By the time of the Midsummer festival, she could no longer see her toenails when standing, though she knew they must be chipped red and less than clean from working barefoot in the orchard for days on end. Still, there were many who saw her on that day and thought she'd never looked better, and a few who told her so.

August: Your baby is the size of an heirloom tomato. An overblown thing, this variety, deep clefts between bloated bulbs of orange flesh. The child might be thriving, but it was not a good year for the vegetable garden. Strange, because the spring rains had been kind, and her friend Peter had boasted that his willow harvest was set to be the best for years. The fields had been rich with cowslips, purple bugle, and even a clutch of green-winged orchids—those bright jesters—brightened the old hay meadow behind the cottage. But the orchard had been slow to blossom and fruit this season. Even the Clarinette, usually plump and knobbly by this time, were warped, and small, and troubled by woolly aphids which she struggled to keep at bay. The late bloomers—Fair Maid of Taunton and Bridgwater Pippin—had barely fruited. And the Kingston Black, the big old tree at the back which bore a heavy cider crop every other year, had failed altogether this spring.

She was saddest about her squashes, which had not fared well alongside their sisters. Over the years she'd tried all sorts—Black Futsu, little pattypans and the garish Turban—and enjoyed them all. But she was best known for the size and sweetness of her butternuts, which she sold in the farmers' market in Wells. This season, though, those big-hearted leaves had sagged from the start, drooping from their stalks like wet sheets. After a few days of rain, the first pale freckles of powdery mildew began to spread from front to back, a dusting of exhaustion for the troubled plants. Then, later, she was forced to crouch awkwardly, enduring kicks of protest, to pick off the refined lemon and ebony carapace of an army of cucumber beetles, which had taken up residence across the bed.

September: Your baby is the size of a large eggplant. The image is set alongside a bowl full of purple-pink flesh with a high sheen. By now, her belly was scored with fine pink lines, and her breasts spilled over even her fullest bras. When the sun was high in the sky, she could do little but sit in the orchard's shade, trying to ignore the scanty crop that hung around her. By night, she slept with all the windows open, but still the warmth and the relentless kicking left her weary and slow by morning.

Some weeks later, though, came a night that brought some relief: a light rain skimmed off the heat of the day, the kicking slowed, and she felt rested when she woke for the first time in many weeks. Later that day, she went walking along the route of the Sweet Track, that strange raised-timber causeway which has given safe passage to six thousand years of travellers through the Avalon Marshes from Shapwick to the Polden Hills.

She walked further than she should have, perhaps, drawn on by the lure of the tor, but she felt fit and strong. When her swollen feet began to pinch a little, she rested amongst the reeds. The bright flags of yellow irises fluttered amongst the green, and she wriggled her toes in the dark water of the channel. She closed her eyes to feel the sunshine on her lids, heard the marsh frogs' laughing chirrup all around.

Even when the cramps started, she didn't panic—she

wasn't disposed to—but retraced her steps across the heath. Stopped now and then, hands around the bloated swell of her belly, willing the pain to end. But by the time she got home, the bleeding was underway, and fear was clutching at her as bad as any cramp.

Peter came, throwing out sheep hurdles and reels of twine from the truck's front seat to make room. He drove her to Musgrove Park and waited until she was admitted. Helped her to a bed in a ward that smelt of gravy and bleach and sadness. He wanted to stay but was shooed away by a fierce midwife with angry red hands.

The next day she found him waiting for her in the badly-lit waiting room, with its Jack Vettriano prints and its view over the back of the incinerator. They sent her off with a plastic package to hold her bloodied clothes, and a handful of leaflets about self-care, and support clinics, and gardens of remembrance. In the truck, she barely heard Peter's stammer as he struggled for the right thing to say. She stared out at the pinking maples lining the high street, the harvest festival banners, the women pushing buggies between busy market stalls. As they waited for the traffic lights to change, the colours merged and swam, and she bit her lip to stop the tears falling.

It was many weeks before she felt able to get out to the garden. It hadn't fared well in her absence. The apple trees were bare, only a handful of windfalls left in the grass. Peter had taken the meagre harvest to the cider mill while she lay in her room, watching patterns thrown onto the white-washed walls by the autumn sun.

In the raised bed, Three Sisters were now down to two: the beans had fallen foul of the snails, which were sliding around their broken corpses even now. The sweetcorn had

49

at least fruited, the silky tassels at the head of each cob just starting to brown. She picked one, twisting the cob hard from the stem so that the whole plant was almost tugged from the soil. The husk was baggier than she would have liked, and when she peeled it back, the kernels were thin and dry, releasing no milk when squeezed.

The squash was an even sorrier sight. Even those blooms that had fruited seemed to have vanished, and the vine was starting to die back already, the leaves discolouring, wilting and deflating so that patches of bare soil were visible once again. She knelt—her belly had started to recede, but it was still an effort—and took her garden knife from her pocket.

She'd almost worked her way through the spent foliage when she saw a flash of cream flesh between the leaves. She sat up then, slashing hard at what was left of the vine, flicking aside a fat, frilled slug which clung to the stem. And then, in the final foot of soil, revealed as she ripped away the last browned leaves, she found a ripe butternut as big as any she'd ever grown. Cushioned by a dent in the soil, its skin was smooth and unblemished. A single tendril curled tightly from where stalk met flesh. The faintest green stripes ran from head to toe, over the bulbous bottom with its ribbed cheeks of flesh, and down to the tight button at the base.

She clipped the stalk with her knife—a single, sharp cut, feeling the prickle of the stem against her fingertips—and lifted the squash. It was warm and so heavy that she had to lean in with both arms to retrieve it. A blackbird began to sing in one of the apple trees—the pretty, bittersweet Chisel Jersey that grew on the bank of the pond. She cradled the great fruit at her elbow, running her fingers over its curves and ridges, marvelling at its weight.

The bird at the pond was joined by another: a robin, singing from the lowest branch of the Sweet Reinette. As they filled the tired garden with their song, she sat back on her heels, shifted the weight a little in the crook of her arm. Stroked the flawless flesh of the squash once more and began to smile.

While the Mynah Bird Watched

When their turn comes, the sun is dipping low, casting long shadows against the pockmarked walls of her consulting room. They've been here before—this man, this girl. Agnes recognises the slump of his shoulders, the sprouting hair at the base of his neck where a shave is overdue, the dusty outline of an old stain on his lapel, under a pin for the city's soccer team. When Agnes motions for them to sit, the man slumps in his chair, as if the air has been stolen from his lungs.

The girl is different. From the outside, her condition manifests itself only through the bald patches across her scalp, and those beads of fever-sweat across her brow. Her hollow cheeks would not mark her out in that waiting room, where malnourishment and anaemia are merely background noise. The bulging masses of her liver and spleen are a secret that only Agnes's tests have revealed. But the girl sits tall in the man-sized chair, her beaded braids swinging even after she is still. Agnes is reminded of someone, long ago, as the girl fixes her across the table with that unbreaking stare. As she grips the desk at the meeting of cracked green leather and well-worn *kiaat* heartwood, knuckles whitening as she presses down on the heavy stitching.

'My wife will come. She must have been held up at the market. Please, wait.' The man is sitting upright now. He has realised that their turn could slip away.

'There is a line. Many to see before I can go home.' Agnes traces the thin skin at her temples, feels the mesh of tendons and skull beneath.

'A minute, please. She will not be long.'

He is right, because the door opens then, revealing a scene of confusion. Ndali is trying to keep a woman from entering, and Agnes can hear the grumble of the queue behind. Another woman, a baby slung over her shoulder like a dishcloth, shouts something from the far side of the hall.

'I'm sorry Doctor, she...' Ndali is doing her best to keep the peace.

'It is fine, Ndali. Madam, please, come in.'

The voices in the hall subside as Ndali ushers the door closed. Agnes sits back in her chair. A police car whines past the window.

'Claudia, where have you been?' the man demands of his wife. There is an angry twitch above his eye.

'A truck hit the water tower. They closed the road. I got off the bus to walk.'

Claudia has not looked at Agnes yet, so she does not know who sits across the table. As she fusses with a scarlet jacket that struggles to contain a spreading waist, Claudia does not know that the woman opposite is recalling a time, long ago. A dusty classroom at lunch recess, the window open wide to the parched air. A mynah bird chattering on a generator lid. A yellow lunch tin splayed on the tiles, and three girls squawking louder than the mynah as they unwrap every one of the careful parcels Agnes's mother has packed.

How they mocked the country food she had grown up with, her headdress with its garish zebra design, and her skin, darker than theirs—almost blue-black—and paint-spattered with the fairy-prints of vitiligo. Claudia was beautiful then. High cheekbones where now there are sagging pouches. Fine, white teeth where now there is yellow rot and holes. Slim, bony fingers where now there are swollen joints, a blackened nail above the thin silver band on her ring finger.

Agnes spreads her own hands across the table. Presses down at the fingertips as the girl did before so that the white patches where pigmentation has been lost stand out even more against the brown. She wonders what will come out when she speaks.

'These drugs, that Maria needs. They are expensive.'

'You can't expect us to pay. We have nothing,' the man says.

'I know that. But you have seen the line. There are many in need. I must think of the rest.'

'She is dying. She must have them. Claudia, you tell her.'

The man's eyes are rolling, red threads across yellow, as he pleads for his daughter's life. But Claudia has seen Agnes now—really seen her—and her mouth sags open. Perhaps she too is thinking of the broken hinges of that lunchbox, and the maize balls crushed underfoot. Of textbooks with fluttering pages as they bump against the brick sides of the well. Of bright spots of red through a sky-blue polo shirt, where the compass point has found its mark.

Claudia stares at Agnes until the doctor meets her eyes at last. Then Claudia looks down. Runs a tongue over cracked lips.

There is a long pause. The man wipes a hand across a

sticky brow. A bluebottle crawls across the windowpane, its legs thick-black and furred. The girl fidgets. Another police car passes, and the patrolman's whistle sounds from the railway stop. The fly buzzes against the glass—suddenly, frantically—its fine gauzy wings grazing the dusted pane. Claudia does not move. Her head still hangs.

When Agnes speaks again, she keeps her body very still. She says what she needs to, and no more. Then, as she writes, she feels her jaw unclench. Her biceps slacken. She feels the tension slide from her shoulders, like the *oshana* that streams through the valley after the rains. She rips the sheet from the pad and hands the prescription to the girl.

As they usher their daughter from the room, Claudia and the man are profuse in their thanks, but Agnes turns away as if she cannot hear them. She keeps her eyes on the photograph propped on the mantelpiece. On the blue sky and the green of the sweet potato vine, the dirt-grey thatch on the homestead where she was born. She lets them blur in front of her eyes until she hears the weighted door pull closed. She does not want them to see her tears.

Collecting Her Thoughts on the Prison Steps

She was always a collector, Ruth. Back at school, it used to be knick-knacks: scented erasers, scrunchies, and those little plastic balls you could fish out of ink cartridges if you had too much time on your hands. We used to swap picture cards from cereal boxes to complete the sets. We were close, Ruth and I, before life got in the way.

Then later, older, and with some money from her job at the Co-op, her tastes changed and grew. Her bedroom and—when she moved out to escape her Dad—her first flat down the bottom of the Arwel Estate were full of cowrie shells, matchbox dioramas, anything and everything with a hippo motif. She wore silver rings on all her fingers: one stacked on another, and more hung on every branch of a little wooden tree beside her bed.

Every year there would be something new: miniature books, ammonites, thimbles; vintage carthen blankets when she was feeling flush; glass bottles—it started with those old ones we used to dig up in the back garden now and then. Pretty soon she had a sizable collection—from antique shops, from bric-a-brac stalls, from that particularly bountiful spot behind the compost heap—and in every colour from deepest medicinal brown through to Bristol blue. She lined them up in height order on the windowsill behind the kitchen sink so that the morning sun flashed the colours across the opposite wall.

Ruth collected men, too, for many years. All sorts. The Barlow brothers, Jacob and Hughie; one not long after the other, though they all seemed happy enough with the arrangement. Then it was Mr Simmons (Junior) from the bank, who looked so uptight we couldn't imagine what they talked about, let alone their lips meeting. For one long summer, she hung around with Iolo Beckett, who wore faded surf shorts and said 'dude' a lot, even though he was nearly forty. Even the quiet lad from the Co-op who did the deliveries: Alun, the one with the port-wine stain on his cheek like a broken heart. She told me that they'd kissed once behind the trolley rack at the end of their shift, that it was the sweetest kiss she'd ever had. It seemed as if she treasured something in all of them.

Ricky put a stop to all that.

They were at a Chamber of Trade dinner, the night they met. Ruth was polishing glasses behind the bar; he was polishing them off on the far side. Ricky was on his best behaviour—charming, as he could be—and afterwards she claimed he made her feel like the belle of the ball.

After they started dating, Ricky humoured her collections, at least for a while. She must have mentioned the hippos because he gave her a little silver one on a chain on their first date. It was hidden in her bread roll, she said, like something from a film. He gave her some bottles for her windowsill, too, though they were new ones from the fancy gift shop in town, and the sharp tints jarred with the faded glamour of the old. In the café of the woollen museum one time—he'd wanted to sell the manager a new till, though there didn't seem much wrong with the old one—she'd admired a framed photograph of some spools of yarn, with brown paper labels spelling out the names: Oatmeal, Scarab and Dark Apple. Robin's Egg, which was the blue she'd always wanted for her room. Never short of money it seemed, Ricky bought it for her there and then.

Back then, I still saw Ruth all the time. In the Co-op of course, but around town too, handbag clinking as always with all the charms she'd strung round the strap. But the changes had already started. She'd taken to wearing her hair scraped back off her face, which added ten years. And though she'd never been much into makeup, now her face was bare, and often there were smudges under her eyes. She'd be smiling still, chatting to everyone she met, but there were times when she wouldn't quite meet my eye.

People had already started talking about the way he treated her. I never witnessed it myself, but I'd not long opened the shop, and I was rarely out of it: business was good, and I couldn't yet afford another pair of hands. Olwen, who'd knocked around with us at school, said she'd seen Ricky shouting at Ruth in the town hall car park—really shouting—until Olwen waved and he stopped and shifted his feet while they said an awkward hello. Someone else, I forget who, said they'd seen him pinch her arm, hard, when she bent to pick up a bundle of old silver spoons from the basket outside the antique shop on the hill. And that she didn't say anything, just dropped the spoons and walked on. Then my mother said she'd heard the two of them going at it hammer and tongs when she walked past the house on the way back from church, one Sunday back in June.

So people had started to talk, and we started to see Ruth around less and less. I kept ringing her, trying to arrange to meet up, but she always had some excuse. She sounded tired. I wish I'd tried harder now, but she always said that she was fine. In fact, I saw him more than I saw her. Though I'd got the shop, I still had a shift in The Crown on a Friday—it kept me in shoes, and I liked Patsy who ran the place—and Ricky used to come in about nine if he was coming. Usually he'd have a couple and then head off before the bell. But once in a while, he'd come in with his eyes red and rheumy, like he'd had a few before he even got in the door. On those nights he'd stay late and want to talk, with an audience gathered around. It seemed he had views on almost everything: migrants ('scroungers'), athletes ('dopers'), whether they should put a barrage across the estuary ('do it, fuck the birds').

I don't know if he knew that Ruth and I were friends, so I don't know if it was deliberate when he started badmouthing her to me. It was a quiet night after an early rush. It was one of *those* nights—he'd come in with his buttons done up wrong, his skin leaching sweat, and one of his eyelids twitching. Without his usual audience, he pulled up a stool and sat right opposite me as I was cleaning the taps.

'Perhaps I should get myself a new girl,' he said, rubbing his thumb up and down his pint. Then he looked straight at me. 'Mine's tired out. Never stops complaining. You'd think she'd know a good thing when she had it, stupid cow.'

Patsy came through the archway right at that moment, called me through to the back bar to clear tables, so that was all I heard that night. I got on the phone straight after my shift, of course, but Ruth didn't pick up, and no answer the next day either. I couldn't stop thinking about her, though, so I shut up the shop at lunchtime and ran down to their house on the edge of town.

It had been Ruth's place before he moved in, and it still

looked like hers from the outside: the cherry tree was hung with all sorts of china birds, and there were old earthenware pots full of pansies on every surface round the slates out the front. The flowers looked parched, though, like they hadn't been watered in weeks, and there was a china bluebird lying on the paving stones under the tree with its little red chest caved in. The bell that had hung on a silver chain below it now lay limp in the dust.

No one answered my knock, and the curtains were pulled, but I had the feeling they were in. That Ruth was, anyway. I called through the letter box, almost lost my fingers over it, but I couldn't prise the slot open far enough to see into the dark hall.

I only noticed the recycling crate as I was opening the gate to leave. Whoever'd thrown the bottles in hadn't cared much for them: dumped from a box, it looked like, and most of them had cracked or shattered. They were all there, though: that handled brown glass jug for Wharton's Whiskey, the squat-shouldered grey carafe of Daffy's Elixir Quack Cure which had sat at the end of the shelf, the miniature soda siphons in soft candy colours which used to light up the kitchen when the sun shone. The simple, clear glass vessels with the heavy collars which she'd dug up in the old vegetable patch were stacked roughly on one side. The flask of Mrs S. A. Allen's World's Hair Restorer, a precious gift from Ruth's American penfriend, had sheared across its deep plum neck. But of her favourite—a square-based bottle with an owl embossed across one face, something from the Owl Drug Company—all that remained was some cobalt blue shards in the crate's grimy base.

A glance back to the curtains and then I reached in to snatch the Wharton's Whiskey and the few soda miniatures which had survived unscathed. I was going to leave it there, but then those blue flashes caught my eye. I wrapped those fractured blue pieces in a tissue as best I could, slipping them into my handbag to run back to the shop.

I didn't give up on Ruth, but my calls always went through to the machine, and the next couple of weeks were hectic at work—trade fairs for the Christmas stock—so I didn't get back to her place. I did drop into the Co-op a few times, but if she was still doing her shifts there, we always seemed to miss each other. I planned to drive up into the city, fit it round some deliveries, to catch her at the office where she used to work two days. But then Olwen said she'd seen her in a park nearby, sitting on a bench on her own, looking well enough. My mother told me to give her time, that she'd come back when she was ready. I told myself I'd wait a month and see.

The weeks rolled by. Ricky came back in the pub; earlier in the week than usual, and it was obvious immediately that he'd been on it a while. A few of the locals were lined up at the bar, and it didn't take him long to pull them all under his spell; as I said, he had charisma of sorts, even when drunk, although by then the sight of him made my flesh creep. That night, he was boasting about being flashed by the cameras down near the bridge, some obnoxious joke about mowing down pensioners. Then he started on about how it didn't matter because his girlfriend would take the points for him. How she'd offered, and he didn't feel he should turn her down, and after all, they needed his car if any money was going to come in. It sounded as if Ruth had dropped the office job, though this was news to me, and she'd always loved it there. Then he made a weak joke about the points and how 'she'd collect anything, that girl', and Kevin and a few of the other regulars laughed because he was buying.

It seemed he was on a run of bad luck, because only a few days later he was back in The Crown with a similar story, though he tried to make out it was Ruth who'd got the points this time, for doing forty in the thirty zone by the school. No one was fooled. Then he muttered something about not being able to pay, which seemed strange seeing as how he'd stood the whole bar a drink the last time he'd been in.

Another few weeks on and Ruth was up in front of the magistrate, being handed out a great big fine, though I never knew it at the time. There was no sign of Ricky for a while, and in the meantime, it seems the fine went unpaid, though the first I heard of it was him lurching in the door one August evening when the bar was sweltering even with the windows thrown as far as they'd go. He looked the worst he'd ever looked: skin like day-old dough, and a vein zigzagging across his temple as if he'd been branded. He was bouncing off chairs and tables just crossing the room; he must have been on it for hours. But he was still cracking jokes about what Ruth might find to collect inside. And then about whether he'd bother to go and collect her when her twelve days were up. No one laughed this time, not even Kevin, who just stared from over by the fruity and then started punching the buttons like he wanted to push them through the back of the machine. Patsy asked Ricky to leave, and you should have seen him protesting like he was the one who'd been wronged.

I drove all the way to Gloucestershire, which is where they send the wicked women of Wales, on the day she was due to be released. Coming down the back roads, past great shifting banks of pink rosebay willowherb, and once-a-year caravanners skidding round the tight bends, I did ask myself what I was doing. But then I remembered that little bluebird with its shattered china chest, and I knew it was the right thing to do.

I had the timings—some online research and a little economy with the truth to a nice lady on the helpline—so I rolled into the prison car park with ten minutes to spare. But half an hour went by, and I started to wonder whether there was a problem. I'd got the day right, I knew that much, because I could see Ricky on the far side of the visitor's car park in that beefed up Beemer he drove like he was on Grand Theft Auto. He was shifting in his seat and winding the window up and down, so I didn't need to see past his shades to guess his patience was wearing thin. No sign of movement behind the big brown gate, though, so there was nothing else to do but wait.

They let her out eventually, with no fanfare. The gate slid half open, and there was a pause for a moment, though I could see arms and activity on the other side. Then Ruth walked out onto the steps, sandals under blue jeans, pale in that yellow cardigan she always wore to cheer herself up. Only two weeks since he'd let her go in there, but autumn had snuck up in the meantime, and her shoulders were hunched with the cold.

And then she stood still—stock still—as if collecting her thoughts on the prison steps. I hadn't expected Ricky to bound up there, but surely even he could have got out of the car? There was no sign that she was looking for him, though. If anything, she was looking at the sky; watching the clouds, which were dense, structural things that day.

Whole landscapes which seemed to seethe and grow while you watched, like milk bubbling over in the pan.

A minute must have passed, and none of us moved. Then, at last, the black door of the Beemer swung open, and Ricky started towards her. He walked like the small man he was, swinging his arms in a suit that was too big for him. When he got close—one hundred yards or so—he shouted: 'Are you coming, or what?'

Nothing.

'I've been sat here a pissing age. They said you'd be out by ten.'

Ruth did look at him, then. She'd put down the leather suitcase she'd carried out with her, with its bright stickers and ribboned handle, but now she picked it up again. I could see that she was spinning the silver rings on the fingers of her other hand like she used to do when we were waiting outside an exam hall. Then she just started walking. Not towards Ricky. Not towards me either, if she'd even seen me, but past my car and straight for the security kiosk on the edge of the car park.

Ricky seemed rooted to the spot, following her with his eyes. Then he started to walk too. Then to jog. To run, chasing her. He was gaining on her, and I knew he'd reach her before the barrier at the car park gate. I'd got my hand to the door handle, but then he stumbled over a kerb. He swore, throwing aside a traffic cone which had been there so long there was a thistle growing out of the top. He didn't start running again. I saw him look up instead, and realised he was looking for cameras, of which there were many, strapped to every other lamp post. So instead he just watched her go: past the kiosk, and then out of sight down the lane which led to the main road.

Ricky was so close to me, I could see the rip in his suit trousers, and the sheen of sweat across his forehead, despite the cold. I couldn't move, but at last he turned and started to walk back towards his car, kicking up stones from the tarmac. That was when I started my engine, swinging out of the car park before he had a chance to get behind the wheel.

She'd got as far as the bus stop. When I wound down the window, Ruth just stared. She was shaking her head as I leaned over to open the door, but then she sank into the seat beside me. It wasn't till she'd pulled the door shut I allowed myself to breathe.

'I've got something for you,' I said, glancing in the wing mirror to make sure there was time. No sign of the Beemer, so I dug into the glove compartment and dropped the package in her lap. A moment to strip away the tissue paper—my eyes flicking up and down to the mirror all the time—and then she held it in her hands: her favourite, the cobalt blue glass even brighter against her pale fingers.

The glue had dried clear, but she must have been able to feel it still, zigzagging between the bright blue shards, standing proud like that angry vein in Ricky's forehead. But she just held the bottle to her lips and kissed it, just where the owl was embossed on its lettered drum.

'Thank you,' she said. And then we started out for home.

Waiting for the Runners

When I reached the bottom of the hill path, there was a pumpkin on the corner, rammed onto the sawn-off lamp post like a head on a stake. A rotting, putrid thing; weeks old. It wasn't even upright—it sagged towards the road, so the tea light inside was a silvery pool of rainwater. The stalk was furring like a baby rabbit's pelt, and the smirking mouth was starting to pucker down at the edges, but I still felt it was laughing at me.

I'd known she'd be there, up at the top, so I'd wanted to be prepared. To get up there before her, so there could be no surprises. Not like that other time: me stood there in an old vest and my painting jeans, watching them leave, not having to wonder too hard why he might want her over me. This time would be different. I'd find a vantage point. Pull a group round me. She wouldn't have the upper hand.

I was later than I'd have liked starting out, though. One of the chickens had woken sickly, stalking the pen like a drunk in search of hooch, and I'd had to wait for the vet to visit at the end of her rounds. Danny always said I was far too soft—he'd have wrung its neck before breakfast—but it's the rest of the flock you have to worry for. Anyhow, it was a false alarm in the end. Just a sore on the wing thanks to that old bully Mabel, no doubt, who takes issue with any challenge to the pecking order.

My heart was thundering as we climbed the path to the top. Arial was bounding up the slope as if he'd just been let out of a box: snapping at leaves, taking great gasps of air, and sniffing at the ivy berries, green and black starbursts like the fireworks last weekend.

When we passed the little allotment at the back of the cottages, the sunflower grove I'd admired there just weeks back now stood sunken-headed and brown. Hunched seed-heads of shame, unharvested and spoilt by the rain. And further up, that stubby-legged pony the children used to call to was standing in a sticky mire around the rusted trough. The ground was greasy there, and I had to grab at the hand-rail to heave myself up the steep bit. I felt my boots slide under me and tried not to yank on Arial's lead. Bright yellow maple leaves fanned across the slick mud; lurid toddler handprints amongst the gritty rust of the beech masts.

She was there first.

Alone, but first. She had her back to me as I rounded the summit, sweat pricking the hair follicles around my face. I paused a moment to get my breath. Right beside the hole Annie used to call the fossil pit, where the cavity left by a fallen tree spills tiny clams and crinoids, and the occasional sea urchin, from its crumbling limestone. There was no time to pore over it today. I lifted the shirt from the small of my back, let the breeze flash cold against my skin. A blackbird flew down from the half-dead oak on the curve of the path, picked at something amongst the leaves, then stopped to stare at me with its unblinking yellow-rimmed eye.

She might turn any moment. I had to walk the final thirty paces and join her at the finish line.

Normally I'd have been delighted for my Benet to have made a new friend. My mother's always saying that he's a strange boy, but he's only different from the splashy men she's drawn to: jazzy trousers and clown specs, comedy turns once they've had a drink. Wouldn't know they'd been slighted, their skin's that rhino-thick. Benet's not like that. He's strong and healthy, never happier than when he's out running, but he's always been delicate when it comes to people. The first to cry after a playgroup scuffle; I don't mean a tantrum—not just some toddler injustice—but a genuine sorrow that he'd been knocked back by another child. He couldn't stand to be told off, was inconsolable if I lost it over the state of the playroom or something broken at home. His sister, Annie, used to tease him sometimes, but she knew when to stop. She could sense his fragile heart.

And then, well... it wasn't surprising really, given how things fell apart. Somewhere along the line, he stopped listening to people in case they said something he didn't like the sound of. Drove his teachers mad. And though he made one friend in junior school—Rob Cowbridge, scrawny little shrimp of a thing—Rob ended up going to the Grammar in town, and Ben had been bobbing about like a lost balloon ever since.

It would have to have been that Will, though, wouldn't it? Not that it was the boy's fault. He seemed a nice enough lad. But *Julie's boy*. Of all the kids to make friends with, to pick the son of your Dad's... well, I hardly knew what to call her now. He'd moved on from her too, I knew that much. She'd lost him just like I had, and with him had gone the smug grin she'd been wearing that day, sitting in the passenger seat while he threw a bagful of threads together and then walked out of our lives for good.

Down in the valley, I could see bonfire smoke coming up from the new-builds where the old factory used to be, though they'd only been lived in a couple of months, so who knew what they'd grown quick enough to burn. I wondered which one was hers. Handy being so near her mum, who still lived in the '60s estate the other side of the stream. But they were tiny houses, those new ones. Close built. Poky, I dare say, if you were used to something much bigger.

He'd been building the place in Stroud for the four of us: Danny, me, Annie and Benet. Julie hadn't been working long as the receptionist in his builder's yard, but time enough to make a connection, it seemed. Then came the day when Annie was hit by a car on her way back from ballet, thrown in the ditch like something fly-tipped. Everything went dark that day, for all of us, and things between Danny and me were never the same after. I dare say Julie was a consoling shoulder, where mine was somehow found wanting.

I was getting close now—couldn't avoid it—but I'd only covered half of the distance between the two of us when there was a great shout from the gorse hedge at the top of the field. Mrs Harris's Lycra thighs emerged from the shrubbery like purple hams. Her neon rash vest and visor followed after, slipping through the gap in the hedge where the stile is.

'Alright, ladies?'

Mrs Harris could out-honk a ship's horn. She was marching down the slope towards us, and that's when Julie—realising she was no longer alone—turned round and saw me.

'They're about five minutes off. You'll not thank me for the state of them, mind, with this mud. Your Benet looks like he's been surfing in the stuff.'

Neither of us replied. If Mrs Harris thought we were rude

for ignoring her, she didn't show it. She just kept on talking: about the state of the ground, about some stray dog, and about how she'd caught a couple of them—naming no names—having a crafty fag round the back of the scout hut halfway round. All the while Julie and I were looking at each other but not looking at each other, like a couple of feral cats.

Mrs Harris was still gabbing on, now about a deer heading off into the old hill fort, when I noticed that Julie hadn't come alone, after all. There was a little girl in a yellow headband hiding round the back of her knees, tracing lines down her mum's skinnies like she was drawing a helter-skelter. I'd forgotten she'd got another one. The girl looked about two years old, with blond curls like wood shavings. I wondered if she was his.

'I'm off back up the track to check them in. You'd better be prepared to make some noise if you're the whole of the welcome party.'

Mrs Harris stamped back up towards the break in the hedge. First time I'd felt like smiling all day, watching that socking great arse trying to hoick itself over the stile. Like a Thelwell pony in spandex.

'You look happy. Can't say I enjoy this much, waiting around knee deep in it.' Julie was pulling at a tab on her quilted jacket while she spoke. *I dare say you don't*, I thought. *I bet you never used to have to do it, either.* This would have been his job, supporting the boy that he swapped for mine.

I could look at her properly now she'd spoken to me. I'd seen her from a distance in the playground, of course. They'd all swarmed round her that first day, like they do when anyone new appears on the scene. She'd brought her mum along for moral support, and the PTA head was in ecstasies at the scent of new blood. That was before they all knew who she was. They might think me hippie and odd and not-their-sort, but the ranks close quickly when an outsider threatens one of their own. Everyone took my side, but even so I'd kept my distance, and we'd never been this close before.

You'll forgive my first reaction, I hope: noticing that time had not been kind to Julie. It gave me a flutter of pleasure to see that those cheekbones had sagged like the melting rim of a church candle. I wasn't unhappy to note that that pretty scattering of freckles across her forehead had now merged into a tea stain of brown. From the way she was thrusting out her chin, it struck me she was trying to hide a fold or two, though God knows we've all got them. But then, and I could have kicked myself for feeling it, there's that sadness in seeing a beautiful woman who's faded, even if you wished all kinds of bad things on them once. I found myself wondering why she wore her hair like that, so that the bare patches at her temples were on show, and why no one had told her about the tidemark of foundation that ran along her jaw.

'They shouldn't be long, now.' My mouth was all wobbly while I was saying it. Malleable, like I couldn't rely on it to do what it was supposed to do. 'I expect we'll hear them coming.'

The little girl was pulling on Julie's coat, and I noticed she had a big plastic ring on her finger. See-through and candy pink, like the one Danny gave me when we had our first wedding: the one in the Juniors' playground at St Peter and St Paul's. So sodding long ago. It must have been springtime because I remember the girls throwing cherry blossom over us before we'd even got started. And Phil Simmons acting the vicar, though he had to go in for his sandwiches before he'd got to the 'man and wife' bit, so perhaps the marriage was on shaky ground from the start.

The little girl had started to come towards me now, and Julie cried out as if she was walking towards a fire.

'Hannah!'

Danny's mother's name. So that answered that one.

'It's okay. I expect she's interested in the dog.' Arial was sitting on the toes of my boots, his tail thumping the wet grass. His eyes were on a rook sat up in a pine tree. 'He's friendly if you want to say hello. He's just watching that bird.'

A great big sigh shuddered up through me. I felt like lying down and rolling away over the turf towards home. What would Julie think of that? Danny's mad wife tumbling face first in the mud like an out-of-control toddler. I expect they used to laugh at me often enough. What was Julie thinking that day, drumming painted fingernails on the steering wheel of her Golf, waiting to take my husband away?

A few more parents were drifting up the path now, some hovering close to us, some hanging back by the fossil pit. The woman with the triplets in year three, who never smiles. Mrs Palmer, Benet's class teacher, with her red setter, Raggie. Mike Hows—such an angry man—was stamping down the remains of a thistle stand as if it'd done him some wrong. And Jackie Fell and Lorna Vaughan were fiddling with their phones while they chatted, never lifting their eyes to each other. There were plenty of glances directed at me and Julie, though. Kay Wellon gave me a look, but I just nodded and turned back to the little girl.

There was nothing of Danny in her face, but there was no

mistaking those curls, and when Hannah smiled at Arial, I saw something there. A memory. Of Annie, strangely enough, which was harder to take. Annie's big lopsided grin when she knew she'd done something right. Lighting the cake candles with a match, like a big girl. Blowing them out for nine, ten, eleven... and then no more.

'He's called Arial, but my son calls him Biscuit. Because he's always trying to eat them. I expect you like biscuits too.'

She didn't answer, but she knelt next to him. Arial let her pat his long black ears, never taking his eyes off the distant bird. I could feel Julie's eyes on me, but I wasn't ready for that yet. I looked at the girl, and I looked at Arial. Then I looked over and down the valley, just as a green woodpecker burst from the shaggy depths of a box tree, trailing its rough laugh as it disappeared out of sight down the hillside.

'Tally ho!' Mrs Harris again, from the far side of the hedge. Then a shout, further away. Laughing, and the crunch of trainers on the rotting maize stalks in the field. Flashes of blue and white where the hedge was thinning. They were on their way.

Mrs Palmer had told me that they did everything together, so it shouldn't have been a surprise that our boys vaulted the stile in quick succession and then ran down the slope towards us arm in arm. Will was kicking something ahead of him: a browning maize cob, trailing what remained of its husk. As they got near, he hoofed it over our heads, and I brushed a strand of rotting silk from my hair.

'We were first. We won!' Benet's navy cotton shorts were lifting above his mud-slicked thighs on each side in turn, baring a white triangle of flesh. His hair was crumpled and damp. His face was flushed, smudged. He still looked like a boy. Julie's Will was taller, his hair shorter, the armband with his race number was tight across his bicep. His lower legs were covered with hair, not the fine down that still dusted Benet's calves. 'Can Will come back to ours?' Ben said, skidding to stop.

'Willy,' the little girl interrupted, saving me from answering as she ran towards her brother. He straightened as if treading water, trying to break his momentum so that she wouldn't be tangled in his long legs.

'Hannah, wait!' Julie snatched her up. And then: 'He could, if you wanted...'

There was a pause, and I thought about that first night after Danny left, when I'd pulled the clothes from every drawer. Buried my face in the rough cable of his Aran sweater until the loose fibres caught the back of my throat. Tipped the chicken pie I'd made for tea—his favourite, for his birthday—into the back pen for the pig.

'Thanks. We have something to do.'

'Fine, just a thought.'

She looked at me then. Her eyes were pink round the lower lids, and there were two short furrows between her brows. I could see her jaw working under the slack skin of her cheek. I thought about my Ben, and how he'd cope if he were on his own again.

'Another time, perhaps,' I said. And she smiled at me so that a delta of lines fanned from the corner of her eyes.

The boys bumped and punched each other as they separated, and then Julie left with her half-grown man and her little girl. The other parents drifted away. Mrs Harris raised her hand as she left with an armful of marker flags. Benet was jumpy and high, but I made him wait, hang back until they were all far down the hill. To distract him, I pointed out the tree where I'd seen the woodpecker. As we stood there, it

75

came back across the hillside—arrow straight between wingbeats, a bolt of green across the valley.

Eventually, I couldn't hold them back any longer, and we set off, Arial sniffing at every stile post, and barking at the poor pony with its sodden coat. I looked at the sloes and reminded myself to return when the first frost had been. Where the path meets the road at the bottom, Benet helped me lift the pumpkin's rotten carcass from the post. We carried it, with its smirking face, to the paddock below the house, and Benet stood on the wall and drop-kicked it across the field. Something changed that day, something eased. When that thing splintered into a hundred coppery pieces across the plough-carved mud, we got free of something. From that day, we started to move forward.

The Day You Asked Me

It was late springtime when you asked me for the first time. The sun was young in the sky, untroubled by cloud, and there were jellyfish everywhere, shrugging and sagging their way through the pea green. My mother barely glanced up from her novel to wave me goodbye, and my father didn't even stir, slumped against the sea wall, black socks snared with sand.

You helped me in from the slatted rocks, handed me a lifejacket, brushed a string of dried petal weed from its industrial zip. Then we sped out to sea, bumping over the breakers at the mouth of the bay, crossing the line of calm where the tides met and dissolved. To where a tumbled mass of slipped shale formed one wall of a tunnel with the cliff-face, just wide enough to embrace a boat in its shade.

In the cool of that cavern, I trailed my hand in the black water, imagining the movement of scale against scale, hide against hide, below us. Of scuttling, of sand flaring up at the touch of a fin. Of anemones pulsing in the dark. The waves swelled and sucked against the rocks, and the boat tipped gently with them. A gull called above us, a rough, hacking caw from somewhere on the cliffs, but then it fell silent, and across the opening we watched its fine-tipped wings roll and arc, and then turn out to sea. It was quiet then, in that hidden place. I watched you, your hands with their bitten nails on the tiller, flecks of peeling skin where the sun had caught the muscles of your arms. Watched you, watching me. We smiled at each other in the dark. I dried my hand on my skirt, reached across to hold yours, tightly. Your lips were paper soft when they touched on mine.

*

Much later, on the day you stood before the altar, summer was closing in, and the church was full of bronzed chrysanthemums, and berries, and sweet-smelling apples in baskets. Your sea-bleached curls had been clipped, but you looked handsome in your thin grey suit, with a pale blue cravat to match your eyes. She wore a veil, studded with tiny lace flowers. Through it, you could see her teeth and the perfect wave of her hair.

I hadn't seen you for years, had been in two minds whether to come at all. Thinking of it simply as a chance to catch up with old friends, I hadn't realised how much it would hurt to see your eyes on hers. Ten years since we'd made promises to each other on the beach before I left for college in the city. I couldn't remember who'd tolled the final bell, but time and space had inserted themselves between us. Taken us too far from the sea.

Now, as the last burn of summer streaked across the dusty air of the church to my pew, I sweated as you swore to hold her till death would you part. I thought about the boy in bare feet in his boat with its crackled red paint and wondered how this had come to be. And at the reception—full of jokes and hard laughter, *Congratulations* in glitter and sequins, little bottles of port with your name and hers handwritten in gold—I crept out the back, past groaning fridges and pallets and trays of cheesecake and meringues.

Blessed the indifference of the motorway to hide my indignant tears.

*

It was autumn when I set eyes on you again, but many years had passed. A cold November day when the fog hung slack across the Severn Vale, loath to lift and let in the weakened sun. The haws were dark in the hedgerows, overripe, and the brambles had turned to a dull, black sludge on their spined stems.

It was the first match for the Under 7s, a festival of sorts. There were boys in mismatched kit from all over, stumbling and rolling for tags, in the shadow of the decommissioned reactor. Saplings tinged with amber and fire ran the length of the razor wire fence, and in front of it the boys—yours and mine amongst them—slithered in the mud and laughed.

You didn't see me, but I knew you from afar. I watched you watch your boy: small, but a good runner. Not afraid to snatch a tag from the bigger boys. I saw you wrap him in your fleeced embrace when he came off in tears of tiredness. Saw you push the blond curls from his eyes, kiss his forehead where the skull cap left it bare. Watched you turn away from me and walk towards your car. I could have called you back, but I let you go again.

*

It was my mother who told me she'd left you. Many more years had gone by. We were by my daughter's bedside, in her tiny cottage, holding her hand while she twisted and cried through the pain of birthing her first child. There were fans of frost on the window panes. Pear-tree logs from the old faithful which had lost its battle with the winds off the moor were spitting in the burner. Two widows, drinking leftover

Christmas Scotch, waiting to welcome the next generation into the world.

My daughter would go quiet for a time now and then, as the baby drew breath. My mother, so old now that her hand in mine was a rigid claw, would fill the gap with gossip: of people I'd forgotten; of people I never knew; of people who had died long ago; and then you.

But it was months, years even, before I thought of it again though, as we lived through my mother's passing. She handed on the baton, but to a new-born who was reluctant to take it. To stay. To live. One hour of staring at a wooden box, then months of staring at a plastic one, willing the little girl in the isolette to hold on. Then those early years of fear, when any sniffle could have us back at the hospital, an oxygen tank looming over her tiny frame. A brave little girl, given her grandmother's name, who will go on to do great things.

*

It is springtime. Dog violets line the stream's mossy path down to the sea. The first of the thrift is dusted along the cliff walk, pale pink splashes amongst the green and grey, and fate has brought us together again. Nursing a cooling cup of tea outside the café on the curve of the sea wall, your brazen terrier runs between my legs, tickling the shin of my good one. I look up to find your eyes on mine.

You wear glasses now, little gold spectacles which frame that same watery blue. Your stick has a fish carved in its walnut head. It reminds me of the weathervane of that church, the ruined one, as it stood at the head of the bay that first day. And you ask me again, though you have no boat now. But you tell me of your son's, just a few yards away. I point to the cast which holds together my crumbling knee. I say a reluctant no.

It's too late.

We left it too long.

Our time is gone.

But you persist. I think again. My daughter is in town, visiting a friend, will not return for several hours yet to fuss over me with rugs and biscuits and old women's things. My son flies in tomorrow when we'll pick him up from the airport to make our annual pilgrimage to his father's grave. But today, today is for you, at last. So I say yes when you ask again. And we wrap my cast in carrier bags, splayed with promises of *value* and *saved pennies* and *being there for you*, laughing at the silliness of it. And I hobble to the harbour wall, where you help me down the steps to the boat, tidier than yours used to be.

We take a trip around the harbour first, while I find my sea legs again. But you're not yet done, and nor am I. Round to that hidden passage through the rocks, where now a young seal—a perfect sheen to its slick head—bobs about at the foot of the cliff. It swims only feet from where you slow the engine and let us drift through the gap in the rocks, through that tunnel of slipped stone. And then we are in, under shale and cliff, and the spring sunshine is tucked away. Mussels cluster between the layers of shale, and the tiny peeping cups of barnacles fit in amongst them.

You let the engine idle in the dark, as you did back then. I can't bend to trail my hand in the water, but I can reach across for yours. I hold it tight, thinking about a life lived apart. And when your paper lips touch mine again, I think of all that I've loved and lost. As a run of waves tips and dips the boat in its swell, you put a hand to steady the tiller, and I wonder what might have been and whether there is anything left for us now.

The House with Three Stories That Might Be Five

Joe and I had planned to come here for our honeymoon, when I had imagined walking under The Queen's Ring with my hand in his, wearing the nine-carat band he'd surprised me with at the Montana State Fair. Back then, I'd assumed we'd grow old together, that one day I'd be tucking some old, red-plaid quilt around his knees, reminiscing about these gardens, asking, *Do you remember the acid green parrot that chattered at the entrance? The Stairway to the Sky, which led you up and then left you, teetering on the edge of the blue? What about the pool where the children were swimming, their warm brown bodies twisting in the spring-fed cold?* We'd be staring out over a yard to a chopped-ice lake beyond, yellowed teeth chattering on the back steps, loose-haired dogs slopped around our ankles. A long way from here, from Las Pozas and the sculptures crowding out from the jungle in this Mexican garden, teasing you with their twisted forms.

We wouldn't grow old and crinkled together, and that's not our yesterday to remember. Our hard-won honeymoon fund ended up in the Church coffers—a loan at first, somehow never repaid. Daniel Windslake could have eased the pocket money from the clammy palm of a toddler. Even that cheap piece of Jewelry World tat, with its tiny solitaire sparkle, found its way across Daniel's palm, via the revolving door of the pawnshop. Still, what I'd give to be there, tucking that quilt round Joe's knee. Instead, I have made my own twisted path, so I must walk it. Even up to the top, where I had walked at Las Pozas this morning, up to where the steps vanish into the jungle air.

'How did you find the gardens, Sally-Ann?' Cathy asks me that night at dinner, out on the bunkhouse terrace. It's cramped for the five of us, hemmed in by dwarf palms and terracotta walls, but the sunset's just visible over the palm thatch, and there's a hummingbird hovering around the splashy red blooms of a planter of autumn sage. Cathy's a college tutor from Brooklyn, not long out of college herself. I had planned to keep to myself on this tour, but since she folded herself into the seat beside me that first day the bus left Tampico, we've got on well enough. Though there is something sad about her, a drooping wilt to her tall frame as if her roots might be too shallow.

Her whole body has paused to wait for my response now, a grilled cob held just out of reach of buttered lips, pale crumbs of Cotija cheese slipping between the rows of hot, plump corns.

The garden of a poet playing God? It felt a little close to home, after everything, I want to say. *I have seen enough of men who think their power knows no bounds.* But even since I'd left Joe, haven't I always wanted to go to Las Pozas, to see the streams tumbling down the slopes amid all that concrete strangeness? I've taken risks, emerging from my enforced solitude, joining this party to make the trip. Crazy risks. But it was worth it.

'It was very special,' I say, if only to make Cathy bite into that dripping cob.

Joe had known nothing of Edward James, of course, eccentric English poet with an eye for the fantastical. Hell, Joe probably couldn't even spell surrealism. But I'd married him for his heart, not his sparks. And today I ended up there without him, in Edward James's Garden of Eden, walking under The Queen's Ring on my lonesome. My ring finger bare, even the tan line long gone from below my knuckle. Is it worth now being safe, if I am always going to be alone?

'*Lengua* taco, Sally-Ann? You have to try it.' Heather's serviette sits untouched on her side-plate, in defiance of the stream of grease that runs from the corner of her mouth and through the funnel of her pocketed chin. 'I thought it'd be a mouthful of rubber bands, but actually it's a real treat.'

'No, thank you. I don't like tongue.'

In fact, we used to eat it often, Joe and I. Not brine-pickled like Mom used to make—greying slabs with a shocking splurge of yellow mustard across them—but braised in a tomato sauce, with carrots bobbing at the top. On the hob till nightfall, when the meat was melting into the gravy. Cheap and simple, when Joe was still a roofer, and I was just starting out as a lowly administrator at the Church, which seemed like a lucky break when I still had college bills to pay. Innocent as a baby back then, I was. No idea of the Church's power, the iron strength of the Gentle Family.

But there is something about Heather, this earnest soil scientist on the vacation of a lifetime, bossy in her mission to share the joy, which draws me to lie. And it comes easy these days, now that I've told so many. Daniel Windslake: this, like so many of my sins, sits at your door.

'Well, you'll have some, Roger, won't you? I saw a woman selling these at a stand on the way up the hill. In goes the filling, pit, pat, toss it on the griddle. Made it look a doddle. And lovely to see such enterprise everywhere we go.'

Roger's sitting at the far end of the table. Free of his floppy sun hat for once, the pink seam of his tan line segments his cheeks and snares the peeling bulb of his nose. 'I'll give it a go, Heather. You know me. Try anything once.'

'I can rely on you, Roger. A man with an adventurous palate.'

'I don't know about that, Heather. But my Rosie always used to say I'd eat a donkey's bollocks laced with arsenic if someone told me it was tasty.'

'Oh, Roger! You are a card. I bet your Rosie had to keep you on a tight leash.'

'She did, Heather. That she did. And I blummin' loved it!'

Heather blushes, pink tickling the grey above her bulbous forehead.

'I'll take that, shall I, Heather?' Peter reaches over from the far side of the table and snatches the rapidly tipping plate from her hand. 'We don't want to lose the rest of the tacos while you flirt with Dodgy Rog here.'

'I wasn't...' Heather blushes deeper, the sweep of rose reaching that mole, with its single hair, which crouches on the side of her neck.

'I know, Heather. Forgive me. I was teasing. I take you as a woman of rather more refined taste.' Peter tucks the loose ends of his paisley scarf away into his shirt so that the silk doesn't stray into the salsa-topped tacos. The flash of skin between the buttons is hairless and waxy pale.

Heather strokes her serviette, looking for reassurance. Oily fingermarks streak dark across the blood-red tissue. Her eyes keep flicking towards the hummingbird as it lingers around the scarlet trumpets of the sage.

'I know fellow composers who would snap you right up, Heather. I'd snap you up myself, but my tastes lie elsewhere, if you know my meaning.'

'Oh gosh, Peter. I won't tell a soul. You can rely on me,' Heather whispers, stage volume, clearly delighted to be entrusted with such secrets. Her cheeks flush with this shiny bead of knowledge in her dull, soil world.

But Peter's declaration comes as no surprise—I've seen the way he looks at Carlos, our carefree driver with wide brown eyes and a deep scar that dances around the crease of his eye socket. Peter's always first to pick out Carlos's sombrero above the other heads in a crowd, to follow the tight crack of his jeans up the concrete steps of the jungle garden. 'I know I can trust you, Heather. We Brits must stick together.'

It's a coach trip, Peter—you'll probably muddle through alone. But she's lapping it up, Roger too. Peter's slippery as an eel: all things for all people. I need to keep my eye on him.

Cathy is still waiting. I've not given her enough yet.

'I've seen pictures of the garden before, of course, but they can't quite convey the way the shapes leap out at you from the forest. The sheer size of it all. A temple to surrealism dropped into the forest like something alien.' I need to stop. Shouldn't have started. But I was an art history major at Carroll College many years ago. There is something in the haunting desolation of the place—stray sunlight winking through a concrete philodendron, the sheer hubris of such a folly. And I've waited so long.

'You sound like you know a thing or two about art?'

See? You'd think I'd have learned to keep my mouth shut by now.

'Oh, it's nothing. Seen a few documentaries, is all. Can I pass you something, Cathy? These meatballs are real good.'

Cathy needs to eat, that's for sure. Her clavicles are sticking through that Dodgers T-shirt like chicken wings. Scrawny ones at that, like the ones we used to pick up from the shack outside Polson. Barely a scrap of meat on them, but the sauce was so good, you'd suck them anyway. With her blue-veined skin, Cathy looks like she hasn't eaten meat for years.

'I'll try the guacamole. My stomach's not so strong. I have to take care with it.'

'You'll be all right with the guacamole, Cathy. Full of lime juice. Keeps the bugs away.'

That's what Mom always said, anyhow. I swear, she'd have washed us in lime juice given half a chance. It should be me taking care of her now—she was weak as a baby bird the last time I saw her. There wasn't even time to say goodbye. Now here I am, eating street food with this strange huddle on a hillside in Mexico, and is she even alive? Daniel Windslake: you have sinned.

'Where you from, Sally-Ann? Sometimes you have the look of someone on the run.'

She's smart, Cathy. I need to watch her too.

'You talking about these clothes? Sure, I can see why you'd think so.'

They'd given me a bag when they dropped me off at the border. Those agents might be good at some stuff, but shopping isn't their forte—looked like a blind man had been let loose in a ten-dollar mall. Some of the dresses are so static, my hair's up like a startled bobcat before I've taken a step. One spark from that grill and I'd go up like the burning bush. Oh, the Church would love that. A fitting end for the whistle-blower, chargrilled by her FBI-crafted disguise.

'Oh no, I didn't mean...'

'S'okay. I had to pack in a hurry. I only got the details for the tour last minute. Found the brochure down the side of an old tram seat in Tampico, and I was here two days later. Everything needed laundering, and there was no time—you know what it's like.'

'Oh sure, sorry. It wasn't your clothes. You just seem on edge. Is everything okay back home?'

How would I know? I haven't seen my husband in five years. Five years tomorrow. He could be at the bottom of Hell Creek for all I know, or romancing that pretty waitress from Old Town Grill in Wolf Point. I don't say it. Of course, I'm hoping he's just sitting on that doorstep, waiting for me to drive up the valley and through that ranch gate like I've never been away, with Mom hollering from the back bedroom that she'd never doubted I'd come home.

'I hope so,' I say. There's a bright green flash of coriander between Cathy's uneven teeth, and I try not to catch my eye on it.

Laughter bursts from the other end of the table, a great splurge of it. Roger is comparing Peter's manicured nails with his own work-ragged claws. Heather's smiling grimly, the chipped remnants of her vacation-treat manicure tucked right into her palms.

'I haven't been home in a long time.' What am I saying? *Stick to the script, you dumb woman.* And yet, being here, the urge to see Joe is so strong, it's almost unbearable. I could call. He could catch a plane. We could walk those steps together at last. Surely they wouldn't be hunting me still, after all this time?

The FBI got most of them the day I ratted them out. Most, but not all, and therein lies the problem. We knew only too well that their poisoned web spread far and wide. The SWAT team caught the Upper Council—but only those who were in town—at their weekly Confessional. Highlight of the week for the superiors of the Gentle Family, watching some poor wretch spilling out all the petty rules he's broken since Sunday, getting thrashed with a horsewhip (and five hundred dollars down) for his trouble.

And Daniel Windslake, of course, was using the time in the way he preferred: giving some special tuition to the confessor's daughter, upstairs in the inner sanctum. Fifteen years old, the officer told me. Barely graduated middle school, just how he liked them. He'd not got all her clothes off yet, so that was something. He was probably in the midst of his speech about gratitude, letting her stroke his gun collection, perhaps, when the guys in black burst in through the fire exit.

Cathy is staring at me now, waiting for more, cob still hanging mid-air. The Cotija has all melted away, a creamy slick amidst the cooling char and yellow.

'It's not good to be alone,' she says, when it's clear I'm not going to offer anything else. 'I should know. I've been alone so long, sometimes I wonder if my reflection might leave me.'

She sinks her incisors into the corns, making buttered juice spurt. I expect her to smile, but she doesn't. I've met all kinds of loneliness, being on the run this long.

*

The jungle is full of birds now, and the light is different from yesterday, cushioned by a mist that still hangs greedily around the treetops. Once wasn't enough: the garden's pulled me back. By now, the others will be at breakfast at the Xilitla bunkhouse, out on that terrace again; Roger tipping down *huevos rancheros* like he's run a marathon since his last meal, not slumped eight hours in a dead-springed bed.

The gates of Las Pozas are only just opening, so I should have the run of the place awhile before the first dazzled tourists wander in. I'm over The Fleur-de-Lys Bridge—concrete grainy with verdant moss—and halfway down to the waterfalls before the sunlight starts to break through. It plays around the steps and arches of The Gate of St Peter and St Paul.

I pick my way through to look down over the pools, but they're empty today, only the splash of white from the falls breaking the still green. Too early for the local boys. They'll be here once school's out. I sit for a while on a bench instead, blue-dyed concrete splattered with orange lichen. There's an empty birdcage on a sawn-off column right in front of me, door sagging open on the hinges, and huge palms all around, flat leaves as big as tablecloths. Tiny, shocking pink flowers stud the forest floor. The birds have quietened since I came close, but one, with this two-note call like a question, just keeps on singing.

They'll be wondering where I am by now. Roger will have finished his breakfast eggs, sunk his grainy coffee, and grown sick of Peter's barbs about his table manners. Cathy will be tapping thin fingers on a glass of passion fruit juice, wanting to get on to the next attraction: the waterfalls of Tamasopo, or Sótano de las Golondrinas. Even Heather will be tiring of the hypnotic, buzzing wings of that hummingbird, ready to get on and see more. But I won't be joining them. I have unfinished business here. There is more for me to see.

I retrace my steps and then walk around the loop, past the

Bathtub Shaped Like an Eye, past a stand of fluid buttresses that hold up nothing at all, and past a gaggle of schoolgirls on the steps of The House of the Flamingos, lounging against the columns as if they need the support. More folk appear as I get closer to the entrance, bemused by their first taste of the garden. I back away, not ready to share it yet, all the way back for one last look at the dizzying steps of The House with Three Stories That Might Be Five.

And then, from nowhere, there he is. On the central platform, looking out over the forest. Joe. My Joe, in a sandy-coloured linen coat I don't recognise, creased around the hem as if he's driven through the night.

'Come and see,' he calls. Sound travels strangely in this place, so his voice is clear across the space, and for a moment I think he's talking to me. 'Come and see,' he says again, turning his head this time. 'That's The Temple of the Ducks, right down there. I thought we'd paddle there later when the sun's warmed up.'

And then she walks out from the shadow of the staircase. Painfully young, even now, five years on. Her hair is braided like the schoolgirl she almost still is. He has his hand at her waist now, and she protests, laughing, at his kiss. He looks happy, younger even, than the night I had to leave.

They start to walk up the exposed steps, concrete planks curling round the monolithic core. I watch him lead, then turn to reassure her, as they climb up towards the sky. I don't have to be any closer to see the tenderness in his eyes. The Gentle Family take with one hand, but they give with the other, and they must know that this is the most poisoned gift they could have given me. He and she climb together, leaving me alone all over again. Up to the top, where the steps vanish into the jungle air.

Breaking the Glass-Blower's Heart

The door closes behind the family, softly, as if the fingers of the person on the other side have lingered on the handle. Then Camila is alone, on her knees amongst the shards of the shattered vase. A bare patch in the dust upon the mantel's leaden-grey marble hints at the vessel's usual position: given pride of place, with its sloping shoulders and its pinched waist. A heart, a glass-blower's heart. Now, some small splinter of glass hunkers under Camila's right shin, threatening to break the skin, as she leans forward to pluck the fragments, one by one, from the reluctant fibres of the rug.

The largest piece is as big as the palm of Camila's hand. It curls up there like a sharp-edged bowl. Blown glass with a swirling bolt of blue; it reminds her of a fresco in the Basilica back home, the many-towered cathedral which dominates the far bank of the Ebro from her mother's tiny flat. Something of the blooming skirts of Goya's Queen of Martyrs captured here in vitreous, bubbled transparency. She thinks back to times when she gazed up at the dome's fresco as a child: sliding along the cathedral's smooth pews with her head tipped back, while her father ran soft cloths over gilt angels, and mopped marble floors around the sandaled feet of the day's last tourists. And then, when what was left of her small clan gathered under the dome for the first *Día de los Muertos* after her father's death, she remembers wondering who would dust the angels now.

There was no question in Joanne's mind as to who smashed the vase, and why. She called Camila—screamed for her—from the front room. Camila had to leave the children alone at the kitchen table. Not that they were concerned: they barely looked up, busily fashioning a rocket from the badly-rinsed contents of the recycling bin.

Tiptoeing amongst the fragments in stockinged feet, Joanne was already at fever pitch by the time Camila came through the door. It was a fight about much more than the vase, of course, but that alone could have done it. Camila has no idea how she provoked it, but distrust has festered between them from the start. Since the day Camila arrived, Joanne has winced if the girl so much as looks at her work, her shoulders hunching as if judgment has fallen before Camila has had a chance to say a word.

Ironically, Joanne's artistry is the one thing she admires about the older woman, most of all the blown glasswork which emerges like crystalline mysteries from the iron-roofed workshop at the end of the lawn. Left alone, Camila has often run her fingertips over ripple-edged vases and bowls, and over those strange, interconnecting forms— purple, bleeding into green, bleeding into blue—brittle sea creatures worn smooth and stranded on the piano's lid.

Joanne was just drawing breath—the eye of the storm— when the two women heard a squeal; the screech of the table's feet across the slate tiles, and the muffled thuds of two sets of footsteps up the few stairs from the kitchen.

'She broke it...'

'It was mine. He took it...'

'I had it first...'

'No...'

Camila's arm shot out without thinking, a barrier across the entrance, preventing the children from straying onto the broken glass. Owen began to squirm at once, never content to be contained. Beca's shoulders were shuddering with tears. Camila bent to squeeze them still, and the little girl nuzzled into her neck. Joanne was frozen, mutely pained, the field of glass between her and hers.

'David.' Joanne broke her silence to yell for her husband. Her eyes didn't leave Camila's. Upstairs, there was the squeak of boards from one side of the ceiling to the other, as David made his way to the landing and down.

It didn't start like this. Should never have turned out like this. The day Camila arrived, the whole family piled up to Stansted to meet the plane. Owen's orange jump-jet T-shirt was the first thing Camila saw when she walked into the arrivals hall, dazed after a bumpy landing and the glass of cheap Tempranillo the businessman beside her had insisted she join him in, before rubbing his fat fingers up her thigh.

The children loved Camila from the moment they met her. They mobbed her, giggling at the brightly foiled *frutas de Aragón* she unwrapped for them, tiny paws pulling at the short lace skirt she was already regretting, as the reality of a British summer's day took hold. David was solicitous: kissing her on both cheeks, snatching up her bag, refusing to take the trolley further. Joanne rolled her eyes, asked about the journey, patted Camila on the arm—stiff, but not yet unfriendly. Camila thought of her mother's enveloping arms and reminded herself that six months would pass quickly.

It was not just that skirt, of course—it became apparent quickly that few of her clothes were suitable. Joanne urged her to go shopping, at her expense; to buy more. (To cover up.) There is no shortage of money here. Whatever David does in that glass-fronted box in the city, it pays for this comfortable Victorian villa. For the fridge with its doors which open like an embrace. For the sleek car on the pavement outside, which is treated to waxes and steam-cleans as if it were some pampered pet. And for her, Camila, of course; David has paid her well. She has sent home €400 each month, leaving tear stains on the letters her mother has sent in reply. But despite Joanne's fluttered notes and hints, Camila has found herself hardening to the weather. Donning tough soled boots under floating dresses as a sole concession to autumn's approach. Even folding that lace skirt over at the waist so that the lower half of her thighs, still deep copper from a summer spent waitressing in a Tarragona beach café, are bare to the breeze.

She and David were thrown together from the start. He likes to be home to bathe the children each night, and Camila, unsure whether it was her place to do so, got into the habit of kneeling by his side. Only rarely did Joanne displace her. Joanne's working hours are erratic, so the children would sometimes go days without seeing their mother, and Camila found herself offering cuddles and kisses in compensation. Joanne blamed the tyranny of the glass. When using moulds, she preferred to cast at night, she said, free from distractions. And the concentration required for free-form sculpting left her exhausted and vague, wandering through the kitchen in her heavy overalls, calipers or a length of blowpipe still clasped in one grey Kevlar mitt.

Joanne would often miss dinner, leaving Camila and David to eat alone, and then perch later on a stool with a sandwich, answering David's enthusiastic questions—technical queries, about melting points, crimping and annealing, desperate attempts to break the ice—in short, staccato bursts. She is thin, Joanne, painfully so, and on the rare occasions she leaves her long, pale neck unwrapped in scarves, her clavicles stretch her translucent skin whiptight. Camila has never seen them touch each other. Sometimes David reaches a hand towards his wife, but she always skids away under it, as a silk cloth slips over glass.

From time to time in these past months, Joanne has gone away. For a weekend, usually. Some weeks ago, she stayed away for five days. There was no warning, though David spoke of a conference as if it had been long planned. In Joanne's absence, Camila grew bolder, stretching and then breaking the strict rules by which Joanne imposed herself on the household. Camila let the children dress themselves, mixing colours and patterns as they chose, swapping Beca's bland T-shirts and skirts for bright dresses with ruffles and bows, which she found in the midweek market in town. She allowed the children to stay up late, and when David returned from work, delayed by the train, he found them dancing in the formal front room, bouncing on the sofas' plump cushions, their faces flushed and high. He ushered them out, gesturing towards the glassware, but he laughed as he chased them up the stairs.

On those evenings, Camila began to cook food from home: spiced *longaniza* sausages with fried eggs and *migas*, and *almojábanas* pastries flavoured with sugar and anise. When David opened a bottle of wine with dinner, she accepted a second glass. On the night before Joanne's return, he opened a second bottle.

Camila pulls a final fragment of glass from the matting

now. It is cold down here on the floor, as if a void beneath the carpet is sucking the heat from the room. She folds her arms under her small breasts and sits back on her heels. Tiny slivers still glitter amongst the rug's fibres, but they will have to wait for the Hoover's indifferent grasp.

She didn't know—why should she?—that this vase was Joanne's favourite. That it was the first vessel David's wife blew unaided. That the wrap of blue that curled through the heart was drawn from a cobalt cane Joanne chose for her mother's eyes. But he knew.

And it was not Camila who left the door to the front room unlocked, the heart-shaped vase lifted down from its place on the mantelpiece to a side table, where it stood no chance against Beca's exploring fingers and Owen's aeroplane arms. She saw his face when he came in—reluctant, but he was prepared to take the blame. David had stoked this fire.

But Camila didn't let him. Instead, she nodded at Joanne's accusations, let the outburst envelop her, impressed by the heat that had risen in this brittle woman. David, beside her, visibly diminished as his wife spoke; he was weak and insubstantial now. Camila watched him shift his weight from one foot to the other, his fingers fidgeting along the undulations of the radiator behind his back.

And when Joanne finished at last, shoulders slumping with the effort of the invective but still defiant, Camila knelt at her employer's feet. She plucked the first of the fragments, lining them up on a folded newspaper beside her knees, while the family shuffled out around her. Beca slipped free to reach for her, but it was David who pulled the little girl back, shepherding her into the hall. Through the closed door now, there are fragments of a conversation.

Camila hears 'flight' and 'morning'. 'That girl' and 'mistake'. A taxi being booked for an early hour.

Camila picks up the largest shard again, with its drape of spun cobalt inside. She wraps it in a tissue, the blue even more vivid against the white. Sharp edges subdued, she tucks it into the pocket of her skirt. By sunset tomorrow, Camila will be back on the banks of the Ebro, back in the arms of her mother. But she will take with her something from the glass-blower's heart.

A Raft of Silver Corpses

It began with the octopuses.

They started turning up in rock pools, as common-place suddenly as shore crab and blennies; unlikely jellies which half-huddled under the sand, squirting from their siphon if approached. Dogs barked at them, and the octopuses would wave a tentacle back in disdain. Sometimes they'd march out of the pool altogether: crouching outraged on the weeded rocks, bobbing up and down on the bladder-wrack, passing through colour changes from milky white to blood red.

It was all a great joke, at first. Children were delighted with these comedy interlopers, leaning in to watch them prance about in the pools. Garish in their displays, the creatures seemed bizarre, shocking even, amongst the muted gobies and shrimp and even the anemones—snake-lock and beadlet and daisy—which had previously seemed exotic. All sorts of stories emerged: of an octopus juggling with empty periwinkle shells, tossing stones from the pool, stealing a sandwich from a picnic. There was even talk of a girl who made friends with one, letting the creature wrap its tentacle around the thin skin of her wrist, taking it home to live in the bath.

The stories swiftly turned sour when the octopuses began

coming up the beach. Just at night, at first: evening dog-walkers talked of finding them mired in sand right up at the tideline, mantles expanding and contracting, blue blood leaking from their beaks. Then, two were found on the lifeboat slipway in broad daylight, heaving themselves towards the boat shack like old women walking into the wind. One lively specimen made it all the way to the Spar in the clutch of shops set back from the harbour wall. It had backed itself into a gap between the fridges, flashing through colour changes as if it were trying to pass on a message in code. It wasn't a localised phenomenon. There was a full-page picture in *The Times*: a little boy in a *PAW Patrol* T-shirt, stretching out his index finger to meet an outstretched arm.

*

The starfish came next, but they did not come out alive.

Thousands of prickly corpses were thrown up on the beach in a single week, by an unusually savage spring tide. The herring gulls gorged on them, deserting the bins outside the chippie in favour of the soft, yellow underbellies of these beached sea stars. And it wasn't just seabirds: magpies and crows, and even a scrawny buzzard came to feast on the unexpected bounty.

But the birds barely made a dent in the numbers. And even when the Sun, Moon and Earth slipped out of alignment, and the tides receded, the starfish kept coming. Soon, the beach smelt rancid, like a fish shop with the fridges down. One starfish was thrown out with such vehemence, it hit the soft concrete in the latest extension of the sea wall and stuck fast there till the morning. When it fell, it left a five-pointed depression behind.

*

When the fish died, they did so all at once, with a violence that shocked everyone.

As if some tipping point had been reached, their oxygen-starved bodies rose to the surface as one. As luck would have it, it was a perfectly still day: a terrible raft of silver corpses, as far as the eye could see, floated together across the bay.

Repulsed already by the foetid starfish remains, people needed no further reason to avoid the beach. The dog walkers made alternative arrangements to meet up in the woods or by the reservoir. The much-mocked early morning litter-picking parties were suspended: after all, what would they be cleaning the sea for, now? Uncollected, a wedge of plastic fragments began to build in a wide arc at the high tide line, a primary-coloured torc of soft-drink bottles and nurdles. A broken window in the surf shack was left unfixed. And though it was almost May, no attempt was made to recruit a lifeguard for the season.

*

It was usually a battle to get funding for the harbour wall, with the sea defence budget spread so thin these days, no matter how many times council taxes were raised to boost it. As a result, the ancient barricade which had been founded in sturdy granite hewn from the hills behind the village had been maintained with the cheapest brick money could buy. These last months, though, money had somehow been found. No one had asked many questions, not wanting to know what vital service had been cut to allow for the mountain of limestone and concrete riprap which had arrived on vast flatbeds throughout the spring. Faceless men in yellow high-vis had fashioned a rubble fortress along the seafront.

But on the day after the fish died, the village came together beside the lifeguard shack one last time. The school choir gathered on the slipway to sing a song, the children holding tight to their ties, wincing into the wind. Then, with pebbles and cement and their bare, red hands, their parents raised the wall another metre, so they didn't have to see what they had done.

Show Me What You're Made Of

It was one of his things, saying that: 'Show me what you're made of,' jutting his chin. It'd always be said in jest—to the stranger at the bar as he pressed a flaming sambuca into their palm, to the kid he challenged to a race to the end of the beach—but there was always an edge to it, right from the start. He'd said it to her on their first date, challenging her to an arm wrestle on the corner table of The Crown's snug bar. Di could see Ella in the background, doing those *are-you-okay?* waggles with her eyebrows, but she'd been drinking tequila since the news came out about her ex's baby that afternoon. She didn't feel the twist in her arm until the morning, and even then she'd blamed it on the way the spilt spirit made the beer mat slide under her elbow.

Looking back, it had always been there, that edge. When they fought, sometimes Di would catch Michael sitting on his hands, or prising open a fist under the table like he was trying to work his fingernails into a clamped shell. But there was a gentleness about him too... or a controlled stillness, at any rate. You could see it in the way he used to play the guitar with his eyes on the horizon, his fingers drifting over the strings, barely grazing them. And watching him with a leaf beetle crawling across the callouses of his palm was the same: he'd stop whatever he was doing to let that glittered bug take its time. Of course, when you knew he would later tweeze off each of those six fine, articulated legs and lay them alongside the severed carapace of its lime-burnished wings, it tarnished the picture somewhat. Because that was the other thing about Michael: he had to get to the heart of everything.

In the early days of the relationship, there didn't seem anything sinister to it. Odd, sure, but back then it had been as much about the rebuilding as the taking apart. An old Triumph came first—a '78 Bonneville—just a blackened shell when he bought it from the car boot sale at the power station. A violin next, then an old hand-loom they found in the barn behind the cottage, and after that, it was his father's watch. Each had their innards splayed across the workshop floor, faithfully recorded on paper as such, like the exploded schematic in a how-to manual. And then, with varying degrees of success, came the reconstruction.

The motorbike seemed to come easily; they'd ridden it together all the way up to Applecross, where he proposed at the top of the slipway with a ring his mother had lent him. And he repaired the loom so well, they were able to sell it on eBay. But the fragile veneer of the violin did not take so well to the indignity of deconstruction. He wore his father's watch on their wedding day, though the mechanism had not turned since the day he'd released the spring and tipped the brass cogs across the kitchen table. When she joked about it while they waited to greet their guests at the door to the marquee, he gripped her wrist so tightly she was left with a pink welt like a watch strap of her own.

That first winter, he spent a few weeks inside, after squaring up to a bigger man in the pub. But when he came home, he touched her with such exaggerated gentleness she let him back into her bed. He'd lost his job because of the conviction, and afterwards he took to spending hours alone in the workshop, the doors locked behind him. He rarely went anywhere for long, but while he visited his mother in the hospice one morning, Di opened the side door with the key he kept under the log basket. She saw then that his interest had shifted, from the mechanics of repair to something more like an inventory of parts. There were no more of the diagrams like engineer's blueprints. Instead, the constituent parts of whatever had taken his fancy were lined up sentry-like, graded by size and shape, everything with its place. She could acknowledge that there was strange beauty in the order of the thing.

She asked him once, what drove him to break apart so much. What he sought to find in all this deconstruction. She'd chosen her moment carefully: he was back from the hospice with a drink in his hand, and his mother was having one of her better days, not mistaking him for his dead brother, nor screaming for a nurse when he arrived. It was before the miscarriage, so he was gentle around her, often stroking her belly, fanning his wide hands across the taut skin. He started to tell her: how he regretted the deconstruction—the essential violence in it—but that it was a necessary evil: only by breaking it utterly could he get to the heart of a thing. Then the doorbell rang with a delivery for next door, and by the time she got back, she knew from the white knuckles around his glass that she'd regret asking more.

He didn't take the loss of the baby well, coming so soon after his mother's death. They buried them together, in the village graveyard that looked over and down towards the Severn Vale. He'd not wanted anyone there, just the two of them, and the unsmiling undertaker from Murray & Sons. Di had brought a bunch of sweet peas from his mother's wild garden, but Michael kicked over the jar as they were leaving, and she didn't dare stop to right it.

After that, he went out even less than before, and a month went by before she knew he'd be away long enough to open up the workshop again. He'd been so quiet in there—none of the usual orchestra of creak and thud and clang of metal on metal—she was intrigued as to what he was working on. He'd been tender with her those past few weeks, and her thirtieth was a month away. Could it be that he was working on something for her? The first chance she got—it had taken an abscess on his jaw to get him out of the house—she lifted the basket for the key. She'd never been any good at restraint.

To a stranger, that picture in the worktop dust might have seemed like a cartoon. A skeleton drawn for a child to cut and pin for Hallowe'en. But on closer inspection, the viewer would have seen the care with which the bones had been sketched in pen and ink, ordered first by body part and then by height, so that the effect was of a ghastly fence, pitched across the width of the page. So many bones needed a huge sheet: he'd used an architect's drawing pad, pre-printed tracing paper with space for the scale and notes. He must have bought it specially. And as the bones declined in size, coming at last to incus, malleus and stapes—the anvil, hammer and stirrup of the inner ear—beyond them, rendered in the same black ink, was lined up a sad collection of small metal items: two medicinal gold studs and a single hair band. She recognised in the sketch of the band the narrowing in the elastic beside the steel fastening, where it had thinned from overuse. On the far side of the sheet, in the pre-printed box for job title, a name had been rubbed out. It began with D, but she didn't pause to decipher the rest of the grooves left on the greased page. She did snatch up the sheet as she ran for the workshop door. She rolled it clumsily, to shroud those careful, dreadful drawings of all the parts of her. Last to slip under the rough scroll—he had drawn it so finely, it could be only hers—was the bald circle of her wedding ring.

On Old Stones, Old Bones, and Love

'Now I understand why the shepherd died.'

They are queueing alongside the bulging gleam of their coach, trapped in a reservoir of dirty exhaust while they wait to get back on.

'What on earth are you talking about?' Margot can feel the ugly pinch in the skin between her brows as she snaps at him. But these days Norman speaks like a man underwater; too slowly and with exaggerated expressions, as if his eyebrows might try to communicate alone. There was a time when she needed to watch his lips to keep up with the barrel roll of his thoughts. Nowadays, she thinks about rummaging under the back of his jacket, searching for the key to wind him. She doesn't wait for an answer now, turning away to tuck in an escaped strand from the bun she tied so early this morning.

'In the Turner painting, I mean. That one of Stonehenge.' Norman hasn't taken the hint. 'You know it, Marg, I'm sure. All savage skies and dead sheep. Those 'in the know' might argue over whether the shepherd was struck by lightning, or whether he's just Turner's emblem of a violent pagan past. I tell you what I think: the lad just lost the will to live, more like, trying to make his way out of the fucking coach park.'

There's a cough, in front, at the profanity, and Margot

turns back, slightly mollified. She can't abide people who flinch at the use of expletives—it seems a terribly middle-class affliction—and she can't help but feel pleased when they are moved to complain. Norman's amused himself, anyway; the points of his cheeks are flushed. And Margot knows she could at least smile (it would cost nothing), but it makes her itch to see the way the cotton-pleated folds around his eyes are contracting.

'I think you're losing it, dear,' she says instead.

But he just shakes his head, exhaling so that the hairs in his nostrils flutter, and holds out a hand for her to go first up the coach's narrow stair.

They must be about the last ones back on the bus, not that it matters: every one of their overwhelmingly geriatric travel companions has meekly returned to the slots allotted to them at London Victoria this morning. The American couple who can't pronounce Salisbury are already pulling white plastic plates from a hotel hamper across their knees. The two East London matriarchs in the front seats are even quicker off the mark, with crumbs already spilling down their sari and dashiki respectively. Bengal silk and Ghanaian kente come together as their heads meet over a Tupperware pot of something reeking of cumin and sweetness. Margot holds her breath as she passes.

A few rows further back, she slips into the window seat Norman insisted she take—her birthday trip, she must make the most of it—and closes her eyes against the inevitable, alien closeness of his leg on hers. She can hear the deep exhalation as he collapses into the upholstery next to her, and the fine whistle which underpins his breath on hot days. She can smell that underarm staleness which emerges every time the cleaner runs the iron over his shirts. They skirt around each other at home these days, hands touching only fleetingly when cold entices them both towards the Aga rail. It's been three years since his snoring drove her down the hall to the little spare room which overlooks the tulip tree. She presses her knees together now so that her thighs won't spill over to his side.

'Are we waiting for someone?'

The woman opposite, who had been sitting straight-backed as a mannequin pressed into a chair, has turned towards the aisle. She's wearing a tatty pendant made from bottle tops and feathers and tarnished copper plumbing parts, all on a long cord. Later, Norman will no doubt describe it as looking like something strangled and washed up on the high-tide line.

'That young couple, perhaps?' The woman has answered her own question before they can reply. 'I didn't see them get back on.'

And she's right: through the window, Margot can see the couple on the path leading back towards the baleen struts of the visitors' centre. The boy has wrapped his muscled arms around the girl's shoulders, and his chin is resting where her hair parts into two sleek plaits. Did we use to be like that, once, Margot wonders? Staring down at the liver spots on the back of Norman's hand, it's difficult to dredge up the memories. But yes, there was a time when they were rarely apart. For a moment, she experiences a strong physical memory, of Norman's hands on her shoulders, of her pulling his arms around from behind, savouring the warmth of his chest against her back. A beach, somewhere cold: Wales, probably. Cheap, if not cheerful; no need to spend more than necessary, she can hear him saying.

Then the coach driver presses the horn, and the young

couple break apart, laughing. The girl's got her hand to the place where she thinks her heart is, as if that youthful vessel might not cope with the shock of the blast. She turns towards the bus, but the boy pulls her back a moment, presses his lips on hers, one plait caught up in his fingers. We used to kiss like that once, Margot thinks. Urgent, so you could feel the jolt of it run through you.

'Fancy a mint?' Norman's asking, but when Margot looks back wearily, he's not addressing her. He's leaning across towards the woman over the aisle, the knuckles of his other hand white on the hand-rest as if reaching out a lifebuoy for a fallen shipmate. When he offers one to Margot, she declines, but then wishes afterwards she'd accepted; it would have been a welcome distraction from the spit and crunch of mastication beside her ear.

There is more waiting and shuffling when they get to the museum in Salisbury, but it's not so bad: the sun has come out, and in the museum's garden, the borders are full of freesias and agapanthus, dusky honey bees drawn to the purple allium globes in the centre of the bed. Two suited gentlemen are supporting each other down the last step of some other coach, and Margot smiles to watch them, then realises that perhaps they are only ten years older, and yet they are so *very* old.

As she stands in the shadow of Johannes von Stumm's *Goliath*, a vast gatekeeper of granite and glass, it seems impossible that she and Norman could ever be so ancient. Surely it was barely yesterday they were students in Highgate, then not long after, walking the jungle in Ecuador, as if nothing could touch them? Moments, surely, since that wild night—so unlikely now—with the shaman on the riverbank, vomiting wild dreams on ayahuasca.

Swimming together afterwards in the Jurumbaino River, holding hands against the crocodiles. Were there even wilting passion-fruit flowers looped into her hair, or has she made up that bit? She breathes out a laugh, acknowledging the lure of the museum tea shop's tin chairs on the far lawn, wondering how long she will be obliged to feign interest in hand axes and old bones.

'Wilfully stupid,' Norman mutters.

It's the American couple again, a few steps ahead in the queue, still mispronouncing Salisbury as they discuss the buildings they've passed through the town.

She watches Norman thrust a note into the donations box on the threshold, banging it down with the heel of his hand, his frown deepening when the tenner catches in the Perspex chute and is left dangling above the silted coins below. Margot feels a pang of something: it might be sympathy, God forbid it's pity. She touches his hand—because Norman is not too tight at all, never has been—but he doesn't notice. He's already striding on, impatient as if the dusty remnants of those who walked these hills and valleys long ago might not wait a moment longer.

It's cooler inside, and the open rooms come as a relief. She has lost sight of Norman, but the exhibits hold her attention more than she had expected. Alone, she moves from one glass case to the next, pulling her spectacles from her bag to read the cards and marvel at the delicacy of a beaten gold pendant, twelve hundred years old, and a perfect teardrop of jadeite, fashioned by some Neolithic craftsman into a flawless axe-head.

In the Wessex Gallery, she is surprised to come upon the Turner watercolour Norman was so exercised about, and she steps close to see for herself the curious way the man had with light: thunderclouds which seem at once menacing and touched with gold, lightning threaded through sunlight. Beside the fallen shepherd and their stricken fellows, the rest of the flock of sheep graze on, oblivious. The great sarsen stones of the monument seem delicate and other-worldly beneath the raging, chemical sky.

Norman's there on the far side of the gallery when she steps back at last, but he's bent over the resting place of the Amesbury Archer, peering at the skeleton between what remains of his hair. It wasn't such a bad joke, about the shepherd, she thinks. Norman used to be known for his wit. He's moving on now, to examine the ridges in an aurochs' horn. Margot smiles as she turns away.

She's staring down at a mosaic pavement, admiring the drop handles of a water jug motif and wondering whether something similar might work as a bathroom tile, when they hear the thud through the gallery's thin walls. A heavy slump, like the slip of old masonry. There's a commotion in the main hall now, and as Margot steps away from the pavement, one of the receptionists appears in the gallery doorway with her hand to her mouth. Then before the cry for a doctor's even gone up, Norman's moving, disappearing through the doorway at a pace she hasn't seen for years.

If she had to guess, she'd have put money on it being one of the Americans; the man, because there's no immediate sign of him when she reaches the reception hall, and his wife's there with her cap off and a tissue to her nose. But when the murmuring crowd around the desk shifts a moment, Margot sees that she's wrong; it's the larger of the East London dames lying prone—the West African woman, whose gilt earrings chimed with tiny bells when she moved. Now, she is on her back, her eyes closed. The loose fabric of her blue and gold dashiki blouse has feathered out like a doomed parachute, and her face looks pale and waxy against the chestnut polish of the parquet. Beside her, her Indian friend fidgets with the tunic's fabric until its bold print runs straight, then unfurls the fingers of her companion's hand to clutch them with her own. And Norman's on his knees beside the Indian woman, leaning close to say something, laying a hand on her shoulder as he does it. Sometimes, that is all there is left to do.

Afterwards, as they wait for the ambulance to bear the body away, Margot thinks about Norman's hands: they might be draped with loose skin now, and sun-freckled, but there is still so much kindness in them. And as they sit side by side in the coach on the way home, with the upright woman across the aisle asleep behind her gold frames, Margot lifts the armrest between the two of them. She places her palm on the back of Norman's hand, fanning her fingers across his. He blinks, twice, then turns over her palm; traces a finger down the life line, the head line, the line of the heart.

The coach slows as they pass the strange green hillock of Old Sarum, and he leans over to place a kiss on the crinkled skin of her cheek. Once, briefly lost in that Ecuadorian rainforest, they navigated home by the lines in their palms, or so they told their children. There are so many more lines now. She leans against him, grateful for the lines they have travelled together.

Lobster Scissors

She was always a storyteller, my mother. A good mimic, too. A clown, even, when the urge took her. Though like the best clowns, she had a darker side.

The first time I heard her tell this story—the story of the girl—was many years ago, when I had not long left home myself. I remember my brother, Reuben, and I laughing as she conjured up the German couple on the cruise ship who'd told it to her: Herr What-Not, with his awkward cough, and the tight Berliner accent that lent his English a staccato edge; and Frau, with her wincing pretensions, and the blanket she tucked round her knees over dinner, even though the billowing steam of the ship's infernal kitchens made this absurd. This German woman had brought on board a strange pair of pink scissors, which particularly delighted my mother, the only apparent purpose of which was to snip the shell and sever the tendons between the joints of lobster claws. She had watched, fascinated, as the older woman cleaned the blades with the edge of a napkin after their one use, before hanging them back around her neck on their gold chain. The trip had been my mother's first away since Dad's death, and I remember we were pleased to see the return of her smile.

It was never a funny story, but the story of the girl held no horror then. While they navigated the slate waters of the Norwegian fjords in that great behemoth, what Herr and Frau recounted to my mother was little more than a fairy story. A girl lost from a wooded village, who returned years later; subtly changed, her memory gone. The details were few: the village was not named, though apparently it was not the couple's own. They had boarded at Warnemünde, having retired to the seaside resort beside the great port. But the story took place somewhere nearby, they implied. They did not claim to know the girl. Still, drawn by something in the story, my mother sought them out again later in the trip. The couple were elusive, and when she did track them down, the closeness of that night had dispersed, she said, and she did not press them on it.

A spooky story, then. Dark, in the tradition of German fairy tales. But by the time it reached my mother's lips, it was told to us lightly by a woman still in the prime of life, and it was as much about the idiosyncrasies of the source as the fairy tale beneath.

It was twenty years before I heard my mother tell the story again, and much had changed. Her strength had waned, and perhaps for us all, the world had grown darker.

We were in the aquarium down by the docks, the day my mother saw fit to tell the story again. It was a rare day out together. Reuben had taken a day off from the oncology ward to join us, and my oldest, Hannah, had consented to spend a single day apart from her monosyllabic friends. The aquarium was a choice of convenience: only my younger child, Barney, had any real interest in the fish, but it was easy to park and find, and the accessibility of the place meant that, even in the hated wheelchair she used by then for excursions, my mother could maintain the illusion of independence.

When we got there, I liked it more than I expected. There was something soothing in the darkness. Ribbons of light rippled across plaster rocks and combined in lacy arrays over the sleek backs of reef sharks. Plump anemones glistened between fronds of purple weed. But it was a strange place for my mother to retell that old story; I'm not sure why the urge took her. The children were with us, as I said, and Barney, though eleven, was still an impressionable child. Hannah, who at eighteen strained against almost all organised activity, seemed sleepy, half-hypnotised by the play of the light. My mother had positioned herself in front of the curving theatre of the main tank—a performer, always— and behind her, an octopus had suckered itself to the front. What a strange, pustuled star; pink flesh stretched pale across the glass. I remember both the children had wide eyes in the neon glow as she began.

As the story rolled out, I noticed at once that it had grown. The girl disappeared, as before, but as my mother told it now, strange happenings began to occur in her absence. Wells ran dry, and small plagues overtook the village: frogs, red-eyed mice, fat-bodied spiders that entered the ears at night. Crying was heard by woodsmen and poachers—screams sometimes—but the direction was always indistinct, and the girl could never be found. When at last she did emerge, her tongue withered from lack of use, all the clothes had rotted from her body. Unable to explain or forget her ordeal, she went mad, quite mad, and threw herself from the bridge into the river that ran through the village's heart, while it rolled and heaved in unseasonal spate.

This was too much for Barney, of course. And as I ushered

him away towards the warmth and light of the rainforest exhibit, I saw that my mother's words had disturbed others too. My husband Martin was caught in a coughing fit. Reuben was grasping at the rail around the stingray pool as if he might otherwise lose his footing, and Hannah had lost the colour in her cheeks. I put my hand on her arm as I passed.

This was at the time when discussions around my mother's future care had just begun—the illusory independence of the aquarium's wide halls was just that, and Reuben and I had been trying for years to persuade her out of her isolated cottage while she had time to make friends in a new place. Recently, with neighbours ringing us with stories of her wanderings and confusion, we had begun to feel that we had no choice but to intervene.

Now I heard Reuben remonstrating with her before we had got out of earshot, and her unrepentant protest. Barney's distress was an unfortunate by-product of her anger. She resented our encroachment on her privacy, she said. She would defend her independence to the end. I had been feeling guilty about booking a visit to a care home—a small place, with a faded grandeur I thought she'd appreciate, and mature gardens that looked over the estuary—but hearing her fierce denials, and the spiteful words she used against my brother, my heart hardened around the decision. All storytellers elaborate, but this tale had deviated far from its source. There was a lobster in the tank as I walked up towards the light with Barney, its hulking blue-black claws laid lightly on the pebbles, and I thought of that German woman and the strange precision of her scissors, about how she might feel to have her story manipulated in this way.

My mother told the story one more time, though it wasn't

from her lips I heard it. It was a few weeks after we'd moved her into Maple Lodge when the police came knocking. They came late one Sunday night. I was watching a period drama, listening out for Barney's cough. Martin was away with work, and the children had gone up hours earlier, so I slid the chain across to answer the door.

They barely gave me time to write a note for Hannah, to hand a protesting Barney over to a confused and yawning neighbour. The overfed tabby from the big house on the corner stared at me through the wound-up window as the panda car rolled towards the headquarters behind the town hall. When I got there, it became apparent there was to be no charge, for now. They acknowledged my mother's age and the notes that had quickly built up in the care home's file, making reference to unreliability and excitability. Nevertheless, the story she had told had struck a chord.

It is true that I went missing as a girl around the time of a number of unusual events in the town where I grew up. To make any connection between those happenings and my fit of teenage angst would be laughable, but enough of the events were real, provable by reference to the archives of the local rag, that the police had not dismissed my mother's story at once. The bout of scarlet fever, if that's what it was, had closed the primary school for a week or more, and a mouse infestation got into the flour sacks and cost the patisserie on Market Street its profits for a month. A dog, an ugly old mastiff that belonged to the owner of the gun shop in the next town along, came back weeks later with ribbons braided into the short fur of its tail. Bright lights were spotted hovering over the plastics factory up on the hill, though this phenomenon was proved later to be the work of a couple of boys with a stunt kite, torches strapped to its cross spar. Then came the clincher: a dead girl. Rebecca Haynes. We all knew her: she went to the Catholic school in the valley, but she was always in the park with the boys from ours. A dead girl found floating face down at the wooded end of the estuary, just feet from where the Historical Society was reconstructing a Saxon fish weir. And my mother—my own mother—had confessed to the police that she'd always suspected I had something to do with it.

They let me go after an hour or two since there was insufficient evidence for any charge. I was home before Barney even woke, though Hannah was slamming doors and playing Gaga at a volume even the Lady herself would object to, so it was evident that she'd come down and found me gone. For weeks after, I played with the idea of visiting my mother, challenging her on what she'd done. But I found I could not. Even Reuben, the dutiful son, left it the best part of a month before he could bring himself to visit Maple Lodge. Sometimes he seemed angrier than me. When he rang me afterwards, he reported that she was rambling, incoherent, but that she sobered up long enough before he left to say that she'd been joking. She'd wanted to teach me a lesson. She was apologetic but ultimately unrepentant. Perhaps now I would understand how she felt.

I never saw my mother again. I did intend to visit, but Maple Lodge rang the day before I was due to go. They'd found her on the carpet outside her room, though it wasn't clear where she'd been headed, as the corridor led only to the laundry cupboard and the kitchen stores. Her right hand was closed in a fist, and when they prized her fingers apart, they found them wrapped round a tiny pair of pink scissors, hung on a golden chain. In her room was some hand-written poetry—flowery doggerel, in the main—about birds, and cloud forms, and the view from a cruise ship. One strange little piece, more crossed out than left written, about how much she loved her children. The day my mother was buried, rain showers were interspersed with bright spells as if even the weather couldn't make up its mind.

My mother is gone, and the story of the girl is gone with her. She was right in one way; there was more to that story. It didn't happen how she told it, but every story changes with the teller. Ribbons of light over plaster rocks—check as many times as you like, it'll never look quite the same. Her story is gone now, but perhaps one day I'll tell you mine.

The Wetshod Child

It was a strange sort of day when I found her. Summery, but with these sudden chills that would sneak up on you. A queer sort of feeling round the place, like things were on the move. A catcheldy day, as my old Dad would have said—changeable, like, neither one thing nor the other. With the bore due up the river, you never knew what the night might bring.

It'd been a busy week, though, what with the church festival bringing in a coach load more tourists slap at the end of June, and I'd had a family from the caravan park out in the boat all afternoon. A wild goose chase for a pod of dolphins that the Watchet marina boys claimed they'd seen near Steep Holm. We'd not got a sniff of the pod, mind, but the tourists had kept me out later than I'd planned, taking snaps of the cliffs at Kilve beach. I wouldn't have cared any other day, but Sal had me worried. More of that red clover fertility nonsense came for her through the post this week, and there was a new crystal hanging in the kitchen window pane. I didn't like to leave her for long.

She seemed okay, though, if distracted, when I got in. I sat with her awhile, shucked some early peas together, but she wasn't in much of a mood for talking. In the end, I decided to head back to the beach. I'd left the dinghy down by the rocks at the foot of the waterfall when I'd brought the tourists in, and with the bore on the way, I'd started fretting about that and all. So I left Sal staring at a cookbook, like she was reading right through to the grain of the table, and went back down to pull the boat in.

The car park was empty when I got down there, save for old Tom's Focus, and he was outside his fish and chip hut, manhandling its slatted shutters in the half-dark.

'You done for the night, Tom?'

'Aarr. All gone.'

He closed the final shutter and brought the metal clasp down hard.

'Been three lasses playing ducks and drakes out at the end of the reefs for the last hour, so I stayed awhile. Two little 'uns and one girt big dollop. Taken themselves off back to the campsite now, so that's me done.'

'I'm back for my boat.'

'Thought as much. It'll get a hammering down there to-night lest you move it.'

'I'll bring it up to the lew.'

'Aarr. Tie it twice, mind, Lewis. It'll be a big 'un tonight.'

'That's what they're saying. See you up the pub for last orders?'

'Aarr. Dare say. If the wife'll have it.'

The tide was on the turn when I got to the ramp: you could feel the wind twitching as it prepared to shift gear. And there were clouds building out to sea, a great stack of them. Grey lumps jostling for space on the horizon. Copper-stained streaks across the sky, crowding out the light. People call this dimpsey, round here—when the light is fading like a switch turned low.

The beach looked empty enough, and I made my way

across the sand to the waterfall. It was splashing and chuntering to itself, just like always, making the rocks gleam at its feet. The singing started up while I was lifting the dinghy free, but I didn't take notice at first. The Zodiac's heavy enough for one man, and it wasn't till I stood up that I fully took in the sound. Sweet singing, but no words that you could make out. I thought it must be those girls at first, come back for a skinny dip in the dark, but the shallows over the reefs were empty as far as I could see.

Job still needed doing, so I pulled the boat up the beach, well beyond the line of weed and litter that marked the highest tides. Last night's was high enough—a string of net scrags and cola bottles and a still sodden sock marked the furthest paw-prints of the sea.

I tied the Zodiac twice to one of the rings in the wall there, thinking of the old gaffer Tom, and turned to feel the breeze. The singing seemed to be getting louder as the waves rolled in. It can play tricks on you, this beach—the cliffs toss the sound around, so you're never too sure where it's coming from—but this sounded like it came from the rock pools on the far side. So I walked down there, wary of the dying light and no torch in my pocket. I could still see the rocks though, and I could see something else and all. Dark shapes amongst the pools, lying across the biggest stones, and all the time the singing was getting louder.

Crack. A broken piece of a child's bucket under my foot, and the sound rang across the beach. The singing stopped all at once, and I had the sense of a crowd turning towards me. I stopped still, but it was no use. A moment, and then those dark shapes began to slip away. Emerging from pools, and across the banks of bladderwrack, they shifted over the short sandbar into the darkening tide. By the time I'd taken my next breath, they were all gone, and I began to wonder if I'd seen them at all.

I would've left then, wondering about seals and sea morgans, and whether those pills Dr Cabot gave me for my chest were turning my head backwards. I would have left, but for an old gull, a great big bugger, which swooped in from the cliff on the wind. It landed on the rock we always dipped for crabs from when I was a boy, and there was a strange sort of light going on because I could see its bright yellow eye quite clear. It looked my way for a moment, then started pecking at something in the pool there. And then I heard something. Something that sounded for all the world like the cry of a baby. So I ran over there quick as, to see what sort of hunky punk we had here.

*

'Sal!' I shouted as I bumped through the door, the wind tearing up the hill behind me.

'What you got there then?' Sal barely looked up from the table as she said this, but a wriggle in the wrapping must have caught her eye because all at once she was on her feet and eyes bright and snatching the babe from my arms.

'First things first, let's get this stinky oil cloth off you, little mite,' she said, stripping layers off the bundle like a kid with pass the parcel.

I was wondering what we'd wrap her in instead, but it turned out I needn't have worried: seemed Sal had a cubbyhole filled with baby bits of one sort or another, and I'd hardly handed her over before she was primped and rolled and looking like something they'd serve in The Creamery in Minehead. I swear Sal just stopped short at putting a doily across the poor mite's forehead.

'Will I call the police, then?'

Sal was still hunched over the babe, making all sorts of cooing noises, and I didn't get an answer at first.

'Sal, the police? We ought to.'

Sal looked up, her dark eyes on mine, that little bundle in her arms, and we both knew then that we wouldn't. Given to us she was, our little Audrey, and we weren't about to give her back.

We needed a story though. It's a small enough village, and people talk. So we came up with this one about Sal's sister, who was working with the Red Cross in Chad, and how she'd left the child with us for safe keeping. A few people did ask, but we kept the details brief, and soon enough I suppose everyone just started thinking of her as ours, like we did.

She loved the water, Audrey did—wetshod, my Dad would have called her, never happier than when she was having a splash—but the water loved her back, it seemed. Least you could never quite get it off her. You could have her wrapped in a towel for an hour, and her hair would still be dripping when you took it off. Drove Sal mad, trying to get her tidy to go out, and Audrey's hair would still look like she'd just been for a dip in the tub. That would have turned a few heads too, so we didn't go out too much. Did nothing so much as sitting in the garden out the back, watching our little girl in the stream that ran down beyond the veg patch, chasing minnows and splashing stones even when there was frost on the ground.

I was out there one day, trying to tempt Audrey back in from the stream for her tea, when a great rumble of thunder came from the south-west. The wind was building, teasing the apple trees in next door's orchard and plucking the telephone wires like cello strings. The bore was on its way again.

Audrey wasn't in the mood for eating, and she seemed right out of sorts, so I put her to bed soon after. Her room's up the front of the house, but she was all of a skitter with the wind, so I put her down in ours at the back instead, which gets some shelter from the lie of the hill. Heard nothing from her till we came up ourselves a few hours later.

Sal was ahead, but when she got to the top of the stairs, she stopped dead.

'Where is she? Where is she, Lewis?' She grabbed my arm. 'Where's our baby gone?'

The bedside light was still on, but our bed was empty. The window above, which leads onto the flat roof, was opened wide to the wind. Who knew how she'd managed the catch—it was stiff enough for grown-up fingers. And there was a pool of water on the sill—if I didn't know better, I might have thought the rain had blown it in.

'She's not on the roof.' I leant right out, but there was nothing: just the mossy lead and the rip of the wind down the combe towards the sea. The bore was so close now.

'I'll go. I'll find her.' My heart was beating like a set of maracas.

'Don't you dare think to leave me here. We'll find her together.'

*

I heard it said once that of the sixty-nine words in the Lord's Prayer (least in our version), sixty-four of them are Anglo-Saxon, like most of the words from round here. I said all sixty-nine though, and a lot more besides, as we ran and jumped and skidded down those steps, even though I've not seen the inside of a church since Mum and Dad passed on.

Not that it did us much good—seemed like He had other things on his mind.

The wind was whipping up a mischief by now, bending those young maples back two-double, and there were bags and papers and all sorts flying round. You'd have stopped to watch any other time—they were like fine ladies dancing—but I was head down, going like the clappers, rain half blinding and the torch all over the shop as I jumped and scrambled down towards the beach. I lost my footing on the bend and scorched my arse right down to the foot of the ramp, and I heard Sal curse as she skidded to stop in time behind me.

The clouds came off the moon for a moment, just as I was righting myself, and I could see the beach was empty. Empty as my heart was feeling. The tide was on the turn, well beyond the last of the reefs, champing at the bit to come up and do its worst. But there was no sign of a living thing.

'Where is she, Lewis?'

Sal's breathing was fast and shallow. She hiccupped the words as much as said them. She'd assumed Audrey would be here, and I realised I had too; that she'd be down in the shallows paddling, those queer little feet set at a quarter to three like always. Maybe that they would be here too, the dark shapes on the rocks, singing their strange sort of song. But there was no barefoot toddler on the beach tonight. And the only dark shape on the rocks was my boat, tossed there by the tide, somehow snatched loose from its moorings.

'Auds! Audrey!' We were both shouting, but the wind pinched the words away like they were weaker than a baby's cry.

'You stand here, hold the torch,' I said to Sal. 'Hold it up so she can find you.'

I left her and ran over to the pools, to the waterfall, to those big boulders where the cliff slides into the sea. I lifted the dinghy, strong as a madman. Threw it aside, to see if Audrey had hidden under. I ran through the shallows, shouting, hollering, on the hunt for anything floating in the rollers. Nothing. If the sea had taken her, it had taken her good and proper.

I scampered about looking for footprints then, any sign that she'd been here at all. But the moon slipped away like it was teasing me. Sal flicked the torchlight over towards me, but it was a pinprick, worse than useless across that great field of sand. So at last, I just stood, staring round desperately, letting the wind hammer my eardrums. Wondering what we'd done to deserve this drubbin'.

You'd think we'd have run back up to the village then, knocked on doors and got a search party going. She could have been anywhere, I hear you say. You didn't just let her go? But we knew, even then. We knew she'd gone. She'd gone back to where she came from.

I was glad the rain was still hammering down as I made my way back up the beach to Sal because I could lose my tears in it. If it hadn't been for her, I might have slipped into the sea myself, let the bore do its worst, but I had to hold her now, lest I lose her too.

I'd almost reached Sal when I heard the singing coming down from the church. 'Just as the Tide Was A-Flowing'. They had a Sing-a-Thon on tonight, for some charity or other. I expect they loved starting it off with that, with the bore on the way. There must have been a good crowd because the chorus was coming down strong, even with the wind in a fury. *My heart it is by you betrayed, for I do love you dearly.* Coming down strong, like I was meant to hear it. And then, all of a sudden, the wind dipped low, and I heard a faint refrain from my back. The sound of singing from the sand. No words, same tune, like they were replying.

I took Sal's hand, and we stood together to listen while they sang their song. They'd got her alright, Audrey, and it sounded like they were singing for joy. By the time they got to the end, I'd got Sal in my arms, sobbing into my shoulder, and even the rain couldn't hide my tears. Say farewell, I said to myself. Brush yourself down and let the wetshod child go on her way.

The Human Bird

Arthur tightened the straps on his left leg and then the other. He'd worn shorts, not wanting to waste a good pair of trousers—ridiculous, now he thought about it—and the leather was cold and unyielding across his shins. It was no easy task to rotate within the frame and slide his arms through the wings without help, but this was the way it needed to be. Old joints didn't like twisting. A spasm of cramp shot through his elbow before he got both arms in place.

A light breeze was snagging at the canvas already, making it balloon between the struts; the conditions were all but perfect. And now he stood erect: a human bird. Arthur took a breath. Felt the morning air shiver through his lungs. Shuffled his feet and coughed, fiddling with the handholds. He hadn't expected to feel so self-conscious.

At least the hilltop was empty. At his back was a clutch of pines that had been planted to mark the anniversary of Waterloo. Sun-dried cones lay here and there in the meadow grass, out of place amongst field scabious and clover. Before him lay the early-misted lowlands of South Gloucestershire, edged by the ramrod-straight track of the Gloucester–Bristol line, the blue-grey snake of the Severn, and the Black Mountains far beyond.

There was a heart-shaped meadow down there some-where, formed within an oak wood. He'd read about it. Planted by a widower in memory of the wife he loved. A family secret until a hot air balloonist spotted it, sending a photograph to the local rag. Arthur thought how much he'd like to look down on that from the air.

What had he done to mark Ann's passing? Very little, save to keep her grave weed-free. Even at that, he'd been found wanting. Buying gaudy petrol station carnations on the way up to the cemetery, until Mrs Haverthorn from next door had complained at finding the plot 'spoiled' by a spilt vase of cheap flowers. His cheeks had pinked with shame.

The funny thing was, Ann wouldn't have cared a jot. Would have laughed, even. Still, Arthur had been into town for roses every time since and taken with them some of that pretty blue campanula she used to grow in the bed by the back door. He knew he could have done more. That foun-tain she'd always wanted for the garden. Or an apple tree—a sweet Belle de Tours—that would have blossomed for her birthday every spring. Another soft rag of failure across his shoulders.

He looked along the wing now. Waggled his fingers, feel-ing foolish. God, they looked old. Grey-blue veins bulging through creped skin, his wedding ring nestled between limp folds like something lost. He thought of Ann's hands: laced through his own, in a churchyard in Devon; cupped around a baby sparrow that had plunged from its aerial home; cupped around their own baby, when Helen arrived, pink and cross, in the hospital bed in Southmead. Graceful hands, Ann had: she might have been a dancer if she'd been taller. Her hands always put him in mind of that Da Vinci sketch: elegant fingers, pastel-soft skin over taut muscles below.

Da Vinci was where this had all started, back when Arthur was a little boy. It had been a big deal, back then, going up to London as a family to see the small collection which had travelled from a museum in the Italian's home town. Arthur's mother was the driving force: she had studied art before she married. His father wouldn't have come were it not for the ride on the Torbay Express, caught as it stopped off in Bristol en route to Paddington.

His mother had bought a mail-order guidebook in advance. 'The human bird shall take his first flight, filling the world with amazement,' read the quote on the first page. And there they were: the whirligig helicopter, the bat-like glider, and that ornithopter that took its inspiration from the flight of birds. Arthur had never seen anything like it.

At the exhibition, young Arthur had pressed his nose to the glass, poring over the spidery words that spoke of Da Vinci's inspiration from the natural world. 'A bird is an instrument working to mathematical law.' Afterwards, he'd been haunted by those scrawled notes and sketches, poring over them in the half-dark of his room, sketching out his own idea. He'd modelled his creation on a jay; the one that used to hop about under the oak tree in his parents' garden, with its smart camel coat brightened by that famous cerulean flash. He'd loved the jerky, robotic movements of its head as it considered the acorns at its feet, picking one, beak improbably wide to accommodate it. And when the bird flew, at first in a great burst and flurry of wings, and then with soaring grace, he'd admired the fantail of its wings and the flash of white rump as it careered towards the wooded hillside. He'd spent many hours watching from the kitchen window, sketching and planning his maiden flight.

He hadn't got very far with the build on that occasion—a first wing, which then sat unloved on a shelf at the back of the garage, until he was sixteen and they moved from their cottage on the wooded hill to a two-up two-down near Bristol. His father had left them, for reasons never explained, and Arthur's mother, angry and sad, wanted to be nearer her sister in Weston-super-Mare.

Arthur's eyes were watering now; his vision blurring. It was that wind, he told himself. He wished he could bend his arms to reach his handkerchief, but his elbow wouldn't thank him for it.

Months, years had gone by before he'd thought of flying again. It'd been a trip to Malmesbury; a visit to an elderly aunt. Arthur had wandered into the town museum, sent to occupy himself while his mother washed up week-old tea-cups. His eye had been caught at once by an image of a winged man: Eilmer, the flying monk, whose study of the flight of birds led him to build his own wings. Five hundred years before Da Vinci puzzled over his ornithopter, Eilmer's maiden flight from the abbey tower had taken him right over the river, breaking only his legs on the far bank.

Arthur had been inspired. His childhood model had survived the move, but its size rendered it useless for his near-adult frame. He'd dismantled it and rebuilt. Two wings this time; taut bedsheets fanned across the struts instead of the silk that Da Vinci favoured, and the tail that Eilmer had wished for. A real-life ornithopter. Arthur had never tried it out. For a while, the thing hung suspended from his bed-room ceiling, but he kept bumping his head on the wingtips, and his mother complained of the dust. So once again it was banished to a garage, left unloved on the back shelves while he left home for an engineering degree in Cardiff.

The breeze was picking up now. Arthur stamped his feet further apart to steady himself. In the distance, he watched a grey heron: long legs stretched ballerina-straight; fast, shallow wing-beats as it traversed the plain. The bird was flying north-west, perhaps to the wetlands at Slimbridge. That was where their daughter, Helen, used to work, as a warden on the reserve. Helen loved birds like her father—it was something they did together, sitting in the kitchen in Redland, watching goldfinches snatch at Niger seeds from the feeder.

When he had retired from the firm in Bristol, he and Ann had moved back here to be nearer their daughter. She'd been on her way to join them for lunch on the day she had the crash—at her father's suggestion, she had taken one junction of the motorway for speed. When he thought about that, Arthur sometimes wondered why he kept on breathing. He and Ann had seen the tailbacks on the news while they prepared the roast, but the chicken had been cold and greasy by the time the call came to say that her old Polo had been trapped between two juggernauts, and that she'd died before the ambulance had even arrived on the scene.

There was a woman at the clinic who always sought him out: Alice Trimbell. They'd been at school together, though she'd been a prefect and a bully, and they'd not been friends. Even now, she didn't seem to notice that he always tried to avoid her eye. It was a mercy—she never missed an opportunity to tell him—that both of his girls had been snatched quickly; mutual friends had aged decades while they nursed loved ones into the ground. It was true that Ann's cancer had taken them both by surprise with its aggression, making its presence known on a scan one Monday in September, and taking her last breath before the month was out. He'd been numb afterwards, for months, and even then he'd barely shed a tear. He'd wanted to feel more, but he had suspicions that his marriage, like the rest of his life, had been a quiet nothing. Between them, Ann and Helen had held his fragile hopes in the palms of their hands, and now they lay prone like a broken-winged sparrow.

A whole year had passed before he left the house for any length of time. Ivy had begun to insinuate itself between the slats on the porch roof, and next door's cat—recognising that its enemy was weakened—had found dominance over the small birds in the garden. Then one day, he'd surprised himself by walking out of the door. Only to the shop, to buy a newspaper, but it was a start. He hadn't read one since the day before Helen's crash. It was only when he'd got home he noticed the image on the cover, although perhaps his subconscious had been onto it sooner: Leonardo Da Vinci—the Flight of Birds.

Just seeing the sketches again in the paper's feature had relit the fire, and he was sketching in the margin before he'd finished reading the piece. Up in the loft, he retrieved the fragments of the model he'd built in his teens. He'd indulged himself over the winter months, using the thermodynamics from his degree and perfecting a scale drawing of what he planned to build. A thick, chesty cough snared his lungs, and some days he questioned whether he had the strength to go on. But the day he'd begun the construction, a jay had visited the garden, and it seemed like a sign.

'You okay, mate?'

Arthur almost lost his footing. He turned awkwardly, found a man with a Staffie behind him, scratching at the logo on his tracksuit as he stared.

'Haven't you heard, mate, we got aeroplanes that'll do that for you these days?'

The dog was straining at the leash. The man was bent sideways as he grinned at Arthur. One of his front teeth was missing.

'Thanks, I know.' Arthur cursed the bloom across his cheeks.

'Want some company? I'm not in a hurry, even if Vader is.' He yanked at the lead, and the Staffie whimpered.

'I'm alright, thanks. Just minding my own business.'

The man shrugged. Behind him, a great buzzard launched itself from a branch in one of the pines, spreading black and tan wingtips to ride the thermals. They both watched it as it soared over their heads.

'I'll be off, then, if you're sure. Stay safe, mate.'

Arthur watched man and dog climb the stile and disappear into the woods. Moments later, the hoarse croak and hectic wingbeats of a pheasant flushed from cover marked their path down the far slope. Then silence fell again, broken only by the breeze and the soft pat and roll of another fir cone.

*

From his hospital bed, Arthur remembered those last moments. He remembered watching the buzzard against the lifting clouds, taunting him with its effortless flight. He remembered looking out over the fields of the Severn Vale as he started to run. The ground had been rutted and fragile, and the slope had dropped away faster than he expected. Even as he'd stumbled and corrected and staggered on, he'd tried to keep his eyes on the white matchsticks of the twin bridges, the lumpen mass of the disused power station at Oldbury, the purple ribbon of distant hills.

And then there'd been a moment, before the fall, when it had really felt like flying. Arms jolted upwards by the air filling his canvas wings. Feet first dragged and then lifted clear of the damp grass. Sweat dampened hair was cooled by the breeze. He'd flown.

Then, darkness. Voices.

'Bit old for the Flugtag, aren't you, love? Need a bit more Red Bull next time, would be my advice'.

A sharp pain in his arm, something jabbed in the back of his hand.

'Almost took the Staffie with him, I heard. Got him by the ankle just as he was taking off. Nasty landing, mind.'

More darkness, more pain, great waves that ebbed and flowed across his skull.

'Grown man in a pair of shorts always looks a bit strange, if you ask me.'

Louder: 'Says he'll come in tomorrow, see how you're getting on.'

A pause. 'Can you hear me?'

'Mr Chisholm's still out for the count, Terri. This Kev guy said he came back for him. Said he thought he looked weird. All dressed up like Superman or summat. Ended up going back to check on him. Anyhow, if Mr Chisholm wakes up, tell him they couldn't fit Kev in the ambulance, so he'll pop round in the morning.'

'Alright, Mand. Have a good night tonight, love,'

When all was quiet, Arthur opened his eyes: one first, then the other. There was a plaque on the far wall, he could just make it out: 'Presented to Gloucester Royal, 2002'. He'd been here before, too many times. He almost vomited at the memories, or perhaps that was the pain. There was a whole shelf of feelings to choose from, and no doubt he should be choosing shame.

Strange, though. That wasn't what he was feeling at all.

The plaque sat under a picture—a silly thing, no skill in it, just a chintzy cartoon of a baby bird. Still, it reminded him of that Emily Dickinson poem about hope: *'the thing with feathers'*. Ann had liked it so much she'd bought it prin-ted on a fridge magnet. And he wondered if there was something perching in his soul that might want to keep on singing after all. All his life he'd wanted it, and today, for a moment—the sweetest, briefest moment—he had been the human bird. Inside this broken, twisted old body, not worth a jot to anyone, there was something that could fly.

Witches Sail in Eggshells

I was working in a bar on Baggot Street when we met. A grimy old place with newspapers for wallpaper in the toilets, but it was an all-women crew and the craic was fine. The bar was double-stacked with rugby boys that night, after the Leinster game. But this girl just pushed through to stand on the rail in front, leaning right over the counter to whisper her order in my ear.

That moment: her breath down my collar, her kohl-crackled eyelashes on my neck... it was like when you cut an orange with your face up close, and all of your senses are alive with the oil and the juice and the bite. My hands were shaking when I tried to spear an olive for her glass. I found myself wishing I'd had time to repaint my nails, that my shirt wasn't so tatty, that I'd done something about my hair before I came out. But she was gone, anyway. Just grabbed the drink, gave a little snort of a laugh, and slipped away. There was a silver charm on the belt of her jeans; we'd barely even spoken, and already I was burning to look closer.

Much later, when the crowds had cleared, I spotted her in the window booth with a group of lads from the DIY shop on the corner. They were a tightknit crew, but she'd look over now and then, and every time, my cheeks lit up like a stoked fire. When my flatmate, Shauna, came on for the late shift, she picked her out in seconds:

'The sort of girl who'd massage your shoulder while she slid her fingers down the crotch of your boyfriend's jeans,' Shauna said. Then she lifted her eyebrows and went back to pulling Smithwick's for what was left of the rugby crew.

'Oo-ee,' said Meg, the chef, when she came through from the kitchen for a ciggie in the shack out front. 'Now that's the sort of girl who'd say she liked your earrings, and you'd hand them over there and then, even though they belonged to your dead mother.'

And Meg wasn't wrong; it seemed like everyone was bending backwards to impress this girl. The boys at her table were jostling for her eye line, crooning 'Lily the Pink', and rolling out bad impressions of the Taoiseach, of Trump, of Gonzo from the Muppets. One of them tried his hand at magic tricks with a stack of beer mats. At first, the girl was laughing, but her face got stonier while he fumbled. Eventually, he tossed the mats and headed for the gents, all his supposed mates hooting behind him.

Not long after, this girl stood up and left the table too, leaving them all gurning like beached pilchards. She settled at the bar instead, sucking her dirty martini through a steel straw, and we talked a bit, between orders. Kezia was her name. She was apprenticed to a tattoo artist, she said, and she was into Celtic designs. We talked about the Claddagh on my wrist, and she seemed interested in the silkscreen printing I was into at the time. Eventually, Shauna rang the bell and started clearing punters, waving her arms like a goose seeing off a pack of dogs. Kezia slipped off her stool, saying she had to run. I needed to stay and clear up, but she scribbled an address on a beer mat from the floor.

'Shall I?' I asked Meg later. Her shoulders dropped, and she rubbed the spot between her eyes—a long day in the kitchen, I guessed.

'Sometimes you need to shag a stranger,' she said, then she sent the pot washer home and headed back through the double doors to finish the last of the clean down herself.

The time Kezia and I had together, I thought it was everything. We were barely apart. Shauna complained that I was always late on shift, or behind with my half of the cleaning. My mother complained that she never saw me, that I'd *never find a man holed up day and night* (my mother's always painted out the inconvenient parts of me). Meg never complained, just patted my arm when she saw me yawning at the bar.

This girl, though: Kezia's hair gleamed black like charred straw, and her eyes were the bluest I'd ever seen. She was a creature of the night, and if we'd barely got a penny between us, she made sure we still went out in style. Right from the start, my wardrobe was her wardrobe; even the Strokes T-shirt Meg had brought me back from NYC. In return, Kezia presented me with the charm from her belt. A five-pointed star in a circle; a gift from some lad she'd got high with at a Full Moon Party. I could have done without the story about what they did on the beach after.

But Shauna had it right: I couldn't do enough for Kezia. It had only been three months; she had both wardrobe drawers and a front door key. I'd wash her clothes, buy her flowers, run her baths which she lay in until they were cold. I got another tattoo—a Celtic knot—because she liked it. She wouldn't have one herself, and that did make me wonder: she seemed to own my skin as well as hers. But she was dazzling. She could shuffle cards so they flowed like a stream over sand. We'd drink tequila on the scrap of beach at the ferry port, pretending we were in Barcelona. And then some honeyed African spirit, next to the lion shelter in the zoo. When my grandmother died, we had sex in the rain.

Saturday was my day off, so we'd spend it marching round Topshop, trying on all the new stock, falling out of changing rooms half-dressed and howling, and then out of one bar after another. Sometimes we'd get home and cook, so late we weren't even sure what meal it was supposed to be. Omelettes usually, because it covered all bases.

'Witches sail in eggcups,' Kezia said one time, holding up a broken shell to the light. Then she smiled and put her finger in through the jagged lip, pulling it out to suck.

'Gross,' said Shauna, pointing the remote as if she wished she could turn Kezia off. The two of them always bristled; Kezia wasn't good with straight girls. She wasn't so good with anyone but me, truth be told. Sometimes, even we fought, and she couldn't always keep it to words. One time, I caught Meg staring at the finger marks on my upper arm. I couldn't make out her expression, and I wished I'd worn long sleeves to cover them.

When the split came, it hit me hard. We'd been fighting, about space, and money, and the fact that Kezia'd sold my old clarinet to pay her share of the rent. It wasn't pretty: there were claw marks beside the bruises on my arms now. Shauna was talking about moving out, and the boys from the flat below came round one night to complain about the noise.

Kezia would stay out late to punish me, then one night she didn't come home at all. Back the next night, her eyes were glittering. She'd not even shed her coat before she'd crowed about what they'd done together: some girl who'd traded a free tattoo for a night in the sack. Kezia curled up on the couch right beside me, watching my eyes as she bragged. Meg was there for once—unusually, because Kezia had all but frightened her off by then—but that didn't stop Kezia. This girl's girlfriend had watched them, she boasted: the tattoo (and then everything after). A serpent, round her nipple, in a dark green ink called Rotten Lust. Kezia spilled words like a pan overflowing, but I was frozen to the cushions, and it was Meg who had to throw her out. I'd strung her charm on a silver chain, and I watched Kezia snatch it up from the kitchen worktop, giggling as she slammed the door behind her.

It was days before I came out of my room. I skipped three shifts, but even Shauna didn't complain. At one point my mother bustled in and out of the flat, oblivious, muttering about the state of my laundry pile, and Dad's dodgy hip, and did I remember Paul MacBride, who used to be the Head Scout, and now he's a marine surveyor in Wicklow? Meg just held my hand until she left; and then on, while my tears soaked a chromatogram of colour across the pillow.

'I'm so sorry. God, I wish I'd never told you to go near,' Meg said. 'The sort of girl who'd batter your heart like a thrush with a snail on a stone.'

But I barely heard her. I just stared out of the window at the robin on next door's shed roof, punishing myself. Maybe I should have fought harder, I thought, stood up for what we'd had. It seemed to me then that robins had it right: singing out to all who'll listen about what is theirs. For months after, I saw Kezia's lips everywhere: TV ads for cosmetics, movie billboards, in the pucker of an anemone on the aquarium glass.

It was exactly two years before I saw Kezia again: Grand

National weekend (that tenner I'd won with an each-way on Many Clouds the day of the split had been scant compensation). By then, I'd moved on from Baggot Street, started a textiles course at the National College, but that day I'd gone back to the old bar to watch the race with Meg. Meg loved the horses—brought up on a stud farm in County Kildare—so she'd sent home the kitchen crew and she and I ran the hot dog stand at the back of the bar together, watching the big screen and making up backstories for the runners' names. I jogged to the bookies with our tenners: her Vieux Lion Rouge to my Blaklion. Neither brought us any luck—One For Arthur snatched the race in the final furlong—but we laughed all afternoon. It'd been ages since we'd spent time together, and I'd forgotten how easy things were between Meg and me.

We were after a late drink when closing time came, but nothing was open, so Meg offered to cook something at mine. Shauna had finally moved out to be with her boyfriend a few months back, so I'd got the place to myself, a luxury I could ill-afford. Meg's eyebrows flew up when she saw the fridge's empty white racks.

'Sorry, I usually have more in.'

'Is that a corner of cheese at the back? An omelette will do us fine.'

Meg was cracking the shells when Kezia let herself in. Two years, to not even knock?

'Witches sail in eggshells,' I heard Meg say from behind me, and I looked back. She was pounding the shells, hard, with the palm of her hand on the flat of a knife.

Kezia just laughed and flicked one of the pink strands she'd got in her hair now.

'Christ, she's not still trying, is she?' she said, gesturing to Meg. 'Give up, girl. She's just not into you.'

I saw Meg's knuckles whiten on the handle of the glass jug on the counter. Then she started whipping the yolks so hard I thought the whole gloopy mess might fling across the room.

'What do you want, Kezia?' I said, turning back.

She'd already dropped her heels and lain herself the length of the couch. Now she laughed and stretched her toes over the arm. Her toenails were painted this vivid teal, like ten scarabs.

'I guess I missed you.'

The sort of girl who'd turn her heel on a beetle on the path. The sort of girl who'd pose naked for a flaming sambuca. The sort of girl who'd turn up after two years and in minutes have you on your knees, begging to rub her feet. I heard all this. (And then a caricature of my mother, in my other ear: *If you'd only find yourself a nice man. That Paul MacBride won't be single forever, you know.* But I am not my mother's daughter).

Meg didn't say a thing: just her feet on the lino turning away towards the sink. But I heard her this time. And I was over by the front door before I knew what I was at.

'Would I mind?' Kezia said, laughing, after I'd asked her to go. 'You'll regret this.'

She'd got the silver charm strung as an earring now, and as it rolled against the white of her neck, I remembered how her skin felt against my lips. How she tasted. How she used to twine that charred straw hair around my fingers, around my neck.

I leant against the back of the door for a long moment after I'd closed it, until I heard Kezia's heels turn the corner at the end of the hall. The sort of girl who left an echo in a room long after she left. But when I turned around, it was only Meg I wanted to hold.

ACKNOWLEDGEMENTS

I'm so grateful for all the support and encouragement I've had in my writing journey so far. It began with Dr Lucy Windridge (now of Cardiff Metropolitan University), who ran the first writing course I attended and lent me that first spark of inspiration. Thank you to the various writing groups I've been part of since, in Wotton-under-Edge and in Cheltenham, and to the network of writing friends I've made (in person and online), who provide such cheer and motivation throughout this writing circus. Thank you especially to John Holland of Stroud Short Stories, for the first opportunity to read my work aloud and all the support since; likewise, the brilliant team at the Bath Short Story Award—Anna, Jane and Jude—who are always so encouraging, and all the various publications who have hosted many of these stories in their pages. Particular thanks to David Borrowdale at Reflex Press for taking the chance on me and bringing this book to life, and to Laura Pashby, talented photographer and my very good friend, whose beautiful shot graces the cover. And to my family, thanks to you lot too (and don't worry, none of these stories is about you...)

'Hagstone' was first published in Fresher Writing Volume 3, Autumn 2017; 'Piñata': The Mechanics' Institute Review Online, April 2018; 'Inches Apart': The Mechanics' Institute Review Online, May 2017; 'Labour of Love': For Books' Sake Weekend Read, February 2016; 'While the Mynah Bird Watched': Halo Magazine Issue 1, July 2016; 'Waiting for the Runners': TSS Publishing, Autumn 2017; 'The House with Three Stories That Might Be Five' (as 'Las Pozas'): The Woven Tale Press, September 2016; 'Breaking the Glass-Blower's Heart': Bath Short Story Award 2017 Anthology (ed.): Brown Dog Books, November 2017; 'Show Me What You're Made Of': Stroud Short Stories Volume Two (2015–18), August 2018; 'The Wetshod Child': Kindred Magazine, Anchor & Plume Press, Fall/Winter 2015; 'The Human Bird': The Nottingham Review Issue 7, March 2017; 'Witches Sail in Eggshells': Bath Short Story Award 2018 Anthology (ed.): Ad Hoc Fiction, December 2018.